Legacy

MICHELLE DOREY

DEDICATION

To all those who have challenged and encouraged me.

CONTENTS

ACKNOWLEDGMENT

I have never written nor published a book without the guidance and help from Jim Moriarty, my favorite American. I love you dearly.

ONE

Damn! The doors of the car slid shut just as I reached the bottom of the stairs. If I hadn't stopped for that latte, I could have made it and managed to get in at least *half* of the class. The squealing of the subway's wheels as it left the station went through my already aching head like a cold knife. Argh! Why did I let Cerise talk me into those last two gimlets last night? The alcohol was probably still oozing out my pores.

I probably should have flagged a cab but it was near the end of the month. If I hit Mom up for an advance again, it would be the third time this semester. Her lectures had gone from 'disappointed' to nagging; if I ask for more money one more time she'd be well and truly pissed. Nope, taking the subway was the wiser move, in spite of the stench.

When the hand touched my arm from behind I let out a squeak and jumped away. Spinning around, I backed up three steps as I pushed my shoulder bag behind me.

A filthy panhandler, his eyes more bloodshot than mine stared at me obsequiously, his hand held out, palm up. "Spare some change?"

I sighed as I rubbed the sleeve of my jacket where he touched me. Shit, now I was going to have to Purell my hand. I shook my head in resignation as I opened the flap of my bag and dug around while keeping an eye on him. Cerise would have laughed at my bleeding heart. Just last night when a beggar on the street asked for some change she asked if he could break a fifty.

There were precious few bills in my purse but I managed to find a few coins to drop into his gnarly hand. It was then that the stench of his B.O. hit me and my stomach convulsed; it was still pretty queasy from last night's vodka and his smell brought me right to the edge of hurling. Ewww!

"Blessings Ma'am." He shuffled off down the platform as I dug out the Purell and spritzed my hands watching his back.

I wish I had turned away, but I didn't. He was wearing a jacket he probably got out of the dumpster at the Salvation Army, but that's not what made me stare. It was his feet.

He had some kind of beat up sneakers, but he didn't have any socks. His pants were too short and I saw how thin his ankles were. They were beyond thin—he was so skinny. My breath caught in my chest.

"Hey!" I called out to him. "Hey, Mister!" I pawed back into my purse sighing. *Maybe I could put the squeeze on Dad without Mom knowing*, I thought to myself as I pulled out my last five and ten.

The guy had turned around. I gulped a lungful of air and holding the two bills up in my hand stepped up to him.

"I want to give this to you, but you have to make me a promise." I didn't inhale yet.

"Huh?" Okay, this guy wasn't a genius.

"Look," I said, "If I give you this extra money, you have to promise me that you'll buy food with it." I leaned forward a little. "And only something to eat. No booze or drugs. You gotta eat something, Mister."

He cackled. "You just called me 'Mister'." He grinned, and after looking at the mess his teeth were, I wish he hadn't.

"Been a long time since I been called that." He reached out for the money.

I snatched my hand back. "No. You have to promise me. A *real* promise."

His eyes were riveted on the money. "Sure. Cross my heart, hope ta die, alright?" He even did the thing with his fingers across his chest, and held out his hand again.

I shook my head 'No'. "I want a real promise. Swear on…" I paused and looked into his eyes. "Swear on the memory of the person you've loved the most." I have nooo clue where that came from, okay? But it had an effect.

His head rocked back like I had slapped him. "Dorothy?" he said. "I gotta swear on Dorothy?" His eyes misted. "I ain't thought of her in a long time, Ma'am."

"Swear on Dorothy, and get something to eat, okay Mister?"

He kept his eyes downcast. "I swear on Dorothy LaRussa that I'll use this money only to get something to eat." He lifted his head. "Promise." His eyes were filled with sorrow and loss. Looking at his face broke my heart.

"I believe you. Here." I passed the two bills to him and they disappeared.

He cackled at me. "Maybe I'll buy bourbon balls at some chocolate shop, huh?" He waved a hand. "Don't worry. I'll eat pizza." He then smacked his lips. "No! There's a White Castle just a few stops down!" His eyes got soft. "I ain't thought about Dorothy in a long, long time, Ma'am." The forlorn expression was replaced by a smile. Sure, it was wistful and bittersweet, but it was a smile. "God, I loved her." He tipped me a two fingered salute. "Thank you for that memory, Ma'am," and turned away. I watched him approach his next victim, a well heeled corporate woman in a black silk Donna Karan jacket.

Just as the next train's doors closed and pulled out of the station. Damn. I almost laughed. No good deed goes unpunished.

'Ma'am!' Did I look that old? Sure, I didn't have time to

put any make-up on but how many Ma'ams wear Zara leggings with three inch stilettos? I pulled out my Clinique compact and flipped open the mirror. Yeah, I looked like hell. But not like a 'Ma'am' okay? I looked like your average, hung over, 23 year old student in a rush to get to class. That's all.

If it was *really* bad, a visit to one of the doctors up in midtown could straighten it out, no problem. I'll worry about that after I finish school and start auditioning. By then I'd have an agent who would tell me flat out if I needed some work done or not. I was still checking for crow's-feet and laugh lines (none!) when the next train pulled in with its screeches and clatters.

Twenty minutes later I entered the brick brownstone that housed the American Academy of Drama and took a deep breath to clear my head. My heels tocked-tocked on the terrazzo floor, while the sounds of voices raised in reciting scripts drifted from the rooms I raced by. I had only gone two steps up the broad stairway when a voice stopped me cold.

"Miz Swanson?"

Oh damn. I knew that voice. I'd sat across from the Director of the school just last week. With my heart in my throat, I turned and managed a small smile. "Yes, Mr. Morris? Can I see you later? I'm late and I really have to—"

"No. I'm afraid we need to talk. Now. Follow me, if you would be so kind." He pushed the thick framed glasses up his aquiline nose and spun on his heels, the overhead light casting a glare on his bald head as he strode down the hall.

For a moment all I could do was stand there clutching the hand rail and blink. This couldn't be good. The last time I'd sat in that office, he'd given me the lecture about how privileged I was to be attending this exclusive school, and the whole Meisner spiel that 'acting was living truthfully in an imaginary world'. And of all the times for him to be roaming the hall, it just *had* to be when I was running late! Shit!

I trudged down the steps and walked down the corridor into his office, just in time to see him pluck a wilted leaf from the ivy plant on the window sill. His smile was tight under flinty grey eyes that zeroed in on me like a bird of prey. He pulled out the chair in front of the desk and with a slight gesture indicated for me to take a seat.

My muddled mind kicked into high gear. "I'm sorry I'm late for class today. My roommate's mother was in a car accident and I was up late with her at the hospital." Please God, let the acting classes pay off enough for him to buy it. I sat down into the seat and leaned forward, giving my best wide-eyed, innocent look.

"Miss Brady. While it is tragic about your roommate's mother..." With fingers steepled, he placed his forefingers across his lips, and cleared his throat. "Keira, why exactly did you enrol in this school? What is it you want from this program?"

Duh. It was hard not to roll my eyes. "I want to be an actress, of course." Something he was preventing right now, with this crap in his office. I should be in class, or anywhere, but right there.

"And how do you see yourself in that profession?" He genuinely looked perplexed as if he had no idea what his school was all about.

My lips twitched in a smile. This was so obvious, it was dead simple. "Successful. Maybe in Hollywood getting millions for every picture, or a sweet gig on a successful TV series." I shrugged, because it really didn't matter which one. "Either way, my..." I arched an eyebrow, "*profession* would encompass glamour, followed by fans and stalked by paparazzi." I twirled a lock of hair around my finger and shrugged again, already seeing myself on the cover of People magazine. Movies or television, I wasn't picky.

His eyebrows rose above the rim of his glasses, making an accordion of his forehead. "Like a Kardashian, perhaps?"

The grin now spread across my lips. I'd give my eye teeth to be a household name like them. "Well, they *are* pretty famous and rich."

His hand slapped the desk, making me pop back in my chair.

"Wrong! The world doesn't need another Kardashian! The correct answer would have been a reference to the craft, your passion to become another person on the stage." He sighed and pushed the glasses up onto the top of his shiny dome. "Do you know how many students applied for the program this year? We turned hundreds of applicants away. You wouldn't be here except for your parents. I accepted you as a favour to Richard and Susan." He pinched the bridge of his nose and closed his eyes.

My heart was in my mouth but my words rushed past it. "But, Mr. Morris, I *do* like to act. I mean...like I might not have said it *right awaaay*...but it's true." Even to my own ears it rang hollow. There were too many early morning classes, too many scripts to memorize. It was grittier and tougher than even the photography program last year. But if I didn't finish this, what would I do?

He huffed a chuckle and shook his head. "Keira, that's probably the best performance I've seen in a while. I'd like to think that you learned that acting skill here, but even I'm not that delusional to buy it."

Ignoring his sarcasm, I plodded ahead. "Please Mr. Morris. Give me another chance. I'll prove to you I can do this."

He just shook his head and his eyes were downcast. "I'll send a partial refund of the tuition to your parents." He stood up and extended his hand, ending the session.

Oh no. That was the final shot. Mom and Dad would know and then there'd be hell to pay. I pushed myself up and my hand was numb shaking his. "I wish I could say this has been a pleasure but..." My mouth pulled to the side and I tugged my shoulder strap higher.

"Good luck, Keira. I'm sorry this didn't work out for you here." He stepped from behind the desk and his hand rested on my arm for a moment. He actually did sound like he regretted all this, but it was probably having to give the money back to my folks.

"Sure." I shrugged and my face hurt when I smiled. "What is it they say? One door closes but another opens?" The hangover was the least of my problems now. I walked out of his office and down the hall looking at the doors of the classrooms where I'd been just the day before. I wouldn't miss the early mornings or getting chewed out for flubbing my lines anymore. Screw it.

Outside, the morning sun streamed gold across the sidewalk. A Monarch butterfly swooped by and landed on the wrought iron railing next to me. It perched there, gently waving its bright wings as I stepped down the stairs. I stopped and watched it for a few moments and then smiled. It was a harbinger of something better. I just knew it.

As far back as I could remember, I always saw a Monarch just before something special would happen. When I was seven years old I saw one on my way home from school, came through the door to find out Mom and Dad were taking me to Disney World.

"I hope you got something for me, Mister Monarch," I said. "Because I'm having a terrible, horrible, no good, very bad day."

It flapped its wings twice then fluttered away.

The vibration of my phone in my bag was followed by my favourite dance tune. I scooped it out, almost running into a jogger who was racing by.

The screen showed Cerise, my partner in, if not crime, then for sure, drunken debauchery. I smiled when I held it to my ear, remembering the hotties who hit on us the night before.

"Hey girlfriend."

"Hey yourself. How you feeling today? I think I'm still wasted." Her words were a little slurred.

"Think you got it bad? I just got kicked out of school....AGAIN!" It felt good to have a shoulder to cry on. God only knew, my parents wouldn't be sympathetic.

"What? No. Way! Why'd they give you the boot?" Her voice blared and I had to pull the phone away. The hangover was starting over again and between her baying and the air brakes of the buses stopping next to me, the pounding in my head came back full force.

I sighed and for a nano-second tears flooded my vision. "I don't know. Morris caught me coming in late. He reamed me out about this not being the thing for me, my motivations...yadda, yadda." I stood at the corner waiting for the light to change, watching business people in Brooks Brothers suits scurry by like mice on a treadmill.

"What the hell does he know? Sounds like he was bullying you. Maybe you should get a lawyer and sue his sorry ass right to hell and back. He can't just kick you out. You paid a shit load of tuition."

"I wish." I jerked to the side when the person behind me, some Goth teenager in a black hoodie, bumped into me.

"Hey jerk! Watch where you're going! I'm walking here!" he barked at me.

I shook my head, glanced at the green light and continued walking. "It doesn't matter. I'll figure out something. There's got to be more to life than getting up at the crap of dawn and putting up with their bullshit."

"That's the spirit! Hey! We should go out tonight. Console you with multiple Vodka Gimlets. Alcohol therapy's the best."

My stomach rolled at the thought of anything other than soda crackers and maybe marshmallows...big fat, monster marshmallows on top of juicy melon chunks. Still, Cerise had a point. After the first drink, whatever vestige of a hangover I would have would disappear. Maybe those guys would be there. "I'm in. The Underground again?"

"For sure! Catch up with you there at ten-ish?"

"Absolutely! Ciao Baby!" I clicked off and headed down the stairs to the subway, leaving my cares on the street above. I could pick up some Chinese and then pass out for a few hours. If those guys were there, I wouldn't have to worry about buying drinks.

I'd think about what I was going to do with the rest of my life tomorrow.

TWO

When the phone rang the next day, I groaned seeing my mother's name on the display. News travelled fast, especially if it was bad.

"Hi Mom." I wandered into the narrow galley kitchen, rummaging in the fridge for anything edible. This was going to be a call that required some fortification. I wedged the phone between my ear and shoulder and peeled the lid from a container of yogurt.

"Keira! I just heard from Alex Morris. You were kicked out of school, AGAIN!" Her words were like bullets from a machine gun piercing my ear.

My eyes closed for a moment and I slumped down into the kitchen chair. "Yes. I showed up late and he threw me out. Can you believe that? I was doing so well and—"

"You weren't doing well! His email contained a progress report from the instructors there. Keira, you missed fourteen classes! There'd only been fifty six at this point in the curriculum! You blew off a third of your classes!" Her voice was cutting my head in two. Hangovers two days in a row were painful.

"No! That isn't right. Maybe I was late but I didn't miss them entirely. He's exaggerating. I swear, he never wanted me there. It's—"

"Enough!" There was silence for a moment or two followed by a sharp sigh. "You need to come home. Be here tonight at six thirty."

"Tonight's not good. I made plans with Cerise to go to the new Star Wars movie. Maybe, on the weekend?" Actually, it was a lie but there was no way I was getting together with Mom, not until she calmed down. Give her a few days and she'd be all right.

"This isn't a request, Keira. It's a family meeting. Your father and I need to talk to you. And just so you know, the credit card and bank account we set up for you is cancelled. I'm afraid it's going to be a little hard for you to go out with your friends without money."

My mouth fell open and the Kiwi yogurt slid off the spoon that was halfway to my lips. NO MONEY! Holy cow, this was serious. "You can't do that. My name is on those accounts."

She let out a bitter chuckle. "I just did Keira. And another thing...pack your things. I've contacted your landlord and your lease is officially broken. You need to be out of there in three days time for the new tenant."

I leapt out of the chair, striding across the kitchen. She couldn't do this to me! "Does Dad know about this?" My words were short and clipped.

"I know." It was my father's low voice breaking through the blinding rage in my head.

"WHAT? You know?" My eyes opened wide. He was my only ray of hope. Surely he'd take pity on me. I was his little girl, after all. My tone became softer, wheedling even. "Daddy, please. Give me a break, will ya? What am I going to—"

"Just be here, Keira." His voice was followed by a soft click.

The disappointment in his voice brought tears to my eyes. Or was it the fact that I'd lost him as an ally? My mother's voice broke through once more.

"I'll expect you at six thirty, sharp." Sharp, just like her tone.

My jaw tightened. "Oh yeah? How am I supposed to get across town without money? Huh? How's that gonna work out for you?"

"I don't know or care. Walk, if you have to." There was a click, not so gentle this time.

I tossed the phone onto the counter and my hands scraped through my hair. This couldn't be happening! What the hell was wrong with them!

I looked around at my kitchen. Sure it was small and the counter top was ancient and cracked but it was MINE! I'd put the cute little fridge magnets on the old white appliance to jazz it up. Now the yawning jaws of the hippopotamus seemed to be laughing...at me. The loopy necked giraffe cast a knowing sneer my way. Even the sunflower on the tea towels seemed to wilt and fade.

It had taken weeks to find this place! Even though it was a basement apartment, it was in the heart of Greenwich Village. What about the coffee shop down the block, and the organic grocery where they knew me by name?

Tears ran down my face as I went into my bed sitting room and looked around. All of the things I'd bought to imprint ME on this place would be gone soon. The bright yellow throw cushions, the blue paisley comforter, the rug from Mexico. I fell down on the oversized bed and buried my head in the plush pillows.

I hadn't even had time to find my true calling after the acting disaster and I was being forced out? This was all my mother's doing! I'd always been a disappointment to her. Not everyone was cut out to get an MBA like her! And she was one to talk! She didn't even use her education! What a waste. No, she and Dad had that phony restaurant that they supposedly ran. How many people can afford a Maserati, and a home in the Upper East Side on income from a greasy spoon? It was a hobby at best.

Why did I need a job anyway? I was going to inherit their millions, some day. I should be free to pursue my own interests...like them. This was bullshit...that's what it was. She was being totally unreasonable.

I got up and went into the kitchen for my phone. It was almost four o'clock. I only had two and a half hours to come up with a plan—something I could sell them to buy me some time to figure this out. I hit the speed dial for Cerise.

Before it connected, I hung up. She wouldn't have any ideas that would help, who was I kidding? I headed back to my bedroom like a condemned man walking the last mile.

I let out a sigh. I needed to look presentable. The yoga pants and sweatshirt weren't going to cut it with Mom. I rifled in my closet and found a decent silk top and jeans that were clean. I topped off my look with a conservative black wool sweater. Not my favourite, but it would have to do. I dug in my purse for any money for cab fare. I'd ride almost to the house and then walk a few blocks. Let her think I'd walked the whole way. Maybe she'd feel guilty about that one! And so she should!

I sniffed and yanked the top from the hanger.

***

The brownstone home was a sturdy sentinel standing shoulder to shoulder with its contemporaries. How many times had I bounced up the six steps and gone through that set of oak doors? The windows on each side, a cross hatch of panes topped with a stained glass panel peered down at me, the lights inside casting a warm glow. And higher, the set on the right hand side on the second floor where my room was, now darkly curtained.

I gave a couple of raps and then used my key to enter, leaving the freedom of the street behind. Taking a deep breath and squaring my shoulders, I called, "Mom? Dad? I'm here." I was right on time and slightly sweaty from the walk, a fact that

I hoped wouldn't go unnoticed.

My mother was the first to step into the hallway near the door, her feet soundless on the marble floor. Blue eyes, like hard sapphires pierced me, peering from an ivory, smooth complexion, her ruby lips a tight unsmiling line. Her arms folded over her chest and she paused. She was a rock of granite standing straight in her Armani top and tailored pants.

My heart slowed somewhat when I saw Dad appear behind her, still in his golf shirt. He towered over her five foot frame, with an athletic ease but she was the real power in that marriage. He managed a smile and stepped forward to kiss my forehead.

"Hi Keira. Thanks for coming."

I looked up at him through my eyelashes and gave a short nod. As if I had a choice on being there. "Hi Daddy." This was the term I used when I was really in Dutch and needed him on my side. When he looped his arm over my shoulder, drawing me in and steering me down the hallway, it showed some kind of promise.

"We'll have dinner in a little while. First, we need to talk." Mom spun on her heels and strode into the living room.

This was a bad sign right from the start. Normally, she'd lead the way into the kitchen, puttering and making me something to eat or drink. The fact that we were meeting in the living room, like I was some kind of sales person or something, wasn't good. It would take all of my persuasive skills to turn her around this time.

They were already seated side by side on the Chippendale sofa. I sat in one of the two matching chairs facing them. The battle lines were drawn.

"Keira."

My face was a mask, waiting for my mother's opening salvo. I kept my hands clasped together on my lap, so they wouldn't notice the slight tremble there.

"It seems that academic life isn't for you." Her eyes flashed to Dad's and she continued. "Have you got anything to say for yourself?"

I kept my face impassive. "I think Mr. Morris was being unfair. I actually liked acting when I got a chance in class." It wasn't my best comeback but I wanted to see where this was heading.

"Well, you see, if you actually attended class the way you were supposed to, then perhaps you could have developed that talent." Mom leaned forward and laced her fingers together on her knees.

"Maybe another school...maybe one where I could take evening classes? I could get a job." Already, I could see it. I'd work in a boutique and get discounts on clothes and cosmetics. Evening classes could work. At least I wouldn't have to get up at ungodly hours.

"To get a job, you need to show up, Keira—something that's not really in your forte. As far as evening classes...how well did that work out for you in the photography course? Or even in the Social Worker classes? The only job you've ever had was in the dry cleaning store and you couldn't even keep that!" A line formed between her manicured eyebrows and her nostrils flared. Yep, Mom was pissed.

"One personal call on my phone and the old bat running the place had a conniption. She just didn't—"

"Keira!" Dad hunched forward and slapped the table in front of me.

I jerked back, staring at him with wide eyes. He never lost his temper. I'd never seen him do anything like that before.

"Your mother and I are concerned for you. Believe it or not, we don't enjoy this any more than you do! But, something's got to be done. You're like a leaf floating in the breeze without purpose or direction. You're twenty-three and you've never held a job, never completed any course except high school and you squeaked by on that. It's not brains. You've got plenty of that! You just don't have discipline." He sighed, but what was worse was the look he shot Mom. He looked defeated.

Mom leaned forward and placed her hand on my knee. A film of tears covered her eyes. "We have a plan for you. You're going to visit your grandmother in Canada."

I looked at Dad. "When did Grandma move to Canada?"

"No," Dad said, "not Grandma."

"It's my mother. " Mom spoke softly

"Your mother? But isn't she dead?" I gave my head a shake. "You told me she was dead. You said she passed away years ago..."

Mom looked away. "I lied."

THREE

This isn't very funny, Mom. What kind of stupid joke is this?"

Dad was the first to break the silence. "We're serious, Keira."

I stared at my mother as if seeing her for the first time. In all the years I'd known this woman, there'd never been any talk of her mother. When I'd asked about her parents, she'd led me to believe they were dead, and that it was a painful subject that she'd rather not talk about. And now, the truth was out.

"Wait a minute. This is the first I hear about my grandmother and you expect me to just up and leave, go to another country to live with a woman I never even knew existed! Are you on drugs?" My heart was going ninety miles an hour and it was all I could do to just sit there. I wanted to throw something at her—at them, for springing this on me now, of all times, when my life was in tatters!

"Keira! That'll be enough. Don't talk to your mother with that tone of voice." He put his arm around Mom and pulled her close. "This is hard on her as well."

16

A tear trickled from the corner of her eyes and she sniffed. "Look, I'm sorry I never told you about your grandmother. There were reasons, which I'm not going to get into with you right now." She patted Dad's knee and continued, "She lives in Kingston, a small city just north of the border. She sent me a telegram and—"

"What the hell is a telegram?"

Ignoring me, she sighed. "She needs someone to assist her. It's her health." Her hands rose to swipe the tears that welled in her eyes.

Part of me wanted to reach out to comfort her but I was shell shocked from all this. "But why don't you go? It's your mother, after all!"

"She specifically asked for you, Keira."

I continued staring at my mother. "How does she even know about me? I mean, I've never even met her. She never once visited or sent a card on my birthday. Why me, right out of the blue?"

Mom was openly crying now which only made me more confused. She was taking this revelation pretty hard. Wait a minute. I'm the one who had been lied to for 23 years. I should be the one crying! What the hell was going on here?

While I stared at her, Dad got up and strode over to the liquor cabinet. "Anyone else need a drink?" The clink of the bottle against the glass followed.

Mom blew her nose and then pocketed the used tissue before taking the brandy that Dad extended to her before he sat back down. "She knows all about you, Keira."

"What? How?"

Mom's face took on a new shade of guilt and she looked at Dad. "I told her all about you."

"When?"

Mom smiled wanly. "On my seasonal shopping trips with my girlfriends."

I closed my eyes and held out my hand. "Wait. You mean you and your bunch of friends that go on shopping trips four times a year? Your 'Four Seasons' gang?" Now I was starting to get mad. "You and your girlfriends would go and visit your mother? But you wouldn't take me?" I stared at her. "You know, that's pretty heinous."

"Take it easy, Kiera," Dad said. He leaned forward on the couch and put a hand on my knee. "There never was a 'Four Season's Club'. It was a ruse to enable your Mom to get out for a few days every few months without raising your suspicion."

Now my anger faded under this new surprise and my mouth hung open. "No 'Four Seasons Club'."

"That's right."

"No shopping trips to Chicago."

"That's right."

I looked over at Mom. "You never went to LA and Rodeo Drive."

She nodded silently.

I looked over from my mother to my father and back again dumbly as it sunk in. "For all those years?" I said quietly.

Mom's voice was a whisper. "Yes."

"YOU LIED TO ME? FOR ALL THOSE YEARS?" My hands went to my head and I scrunched my hair in my fingers. My mother had led a double life, not even bothering to let me know about my grandmother! And Dad had known all about it! But why? Why keep this from me? I had a right to know.

"You didn't think that maybe, just maybe, I would have liked to meet her? Why did she never come here? You said yourself, it's just north of the border, not half way around the world, for God's sake!" Dad hadn't bothered to get me a drink but I needed one. I got up and went over to the cabinet and poured a stiff one.

"She had her reasons. That's all I'm going to say. You'll find out more when you meet her." My mother took a long swallow of her drink, eyeing me over the rim of her glass. She had collected herself and was once again all business. Every blonde tipped hair on her head was perfectly coiffed. The casual bangles on her wrist tinkled below the cuff of her top. It was all so cut and dried, her pronouncement, just like her everything about her.

"I'm not sure I'm going." I wandered back to the chair, being careful to not spill the drink on her gleaming floors. "I mean, she didn't bother to try to contact me before this and now that she's ill, she wants to get to know me? That's cold."

"Kiera—she's not well." Mom's composure faltered again and her chin quivered. She's very, very old and she's asking for you now." She looked over at Dad and some silent message passed between them and they both nodded and faced me again.

"So I'm supposed to just pack up and go... to Canada and freeze to death and be her nursemaid?"

"Kiera, it's June!"

"It's Canada!"

Now they both started laughing at me, and that got me even more mad. "I've been there! When we went skiing at that Mt. Tremblant place! That's in Canada! It was freezing! And the snow was like really deep!"

"That was a ski resort! There's always deep snow! And it was February!" She wiped her eyes again, but this time from laughing. "The weather's just like here for the most part."

Mom was laughing. At me. Oooh! I folded my arms. "I don't know anything about taking care of old people. Doesn't sound like something I'd want to do, taking care of someone *I don't know.*"

"Oh? I would think you'd *jump* at the chance. This is not only a lifeline for her, but it's one for you as well." Mom's eyes narrowed and she leaned forward, peering at me.

"A lifeline? Nursing an old woman who never cared enough to even *meet* me?" I shook my head and snorted.

Dad leaned forward and held up his hand. "Hold on, Keira. It's not that simple. And, have you considered your other options?" His mouth pulled to the side and he looked at me with sad eyes. "There aren't any. You don't have a job. Don't have money. You don't even have a place to live after the end of the month—which is three days from now."

My mouth fell along with my stomach. "What? I can't stay here until I figure this out?"

He shook his head and my mother sighed. "Nope. I need the keys to the townhouse back. If you don't agree to help your grandmother, you're on your own."

This time, it was *my* eyes that filled with tears. How could they do this to me? My whole world had slipped off its axis.

FOUR

The next couple of days passed in a horrid nightmare. My apartment was packed up and cleaned out and now consisted of bulging boxes in the basement of the townhouse. 'The last supper' was a solemn affair with none of us terribly talkative. I was still fuming over the trip north the next morning and my parents were probably feeling a little guilty about this whole affair. At least I hoped they were.

It was Mom who drove me to the airport. That was no surprise as Dad didn't do well with emotional goodbyes. The streets flew by as she handled the Maserati like a race car driver. It was probably futile but I had to give it one more shot.

"Mom, I think you'd be better to go see Grandmother and take care of her. I mean, you know her, whereas I'm a total stranger. Considering her age, maybe that would be easier on her. I can look after Dad and put out some resumes to find a job while you're gone." We were only five minutes out from LaGuardia and time was slipping away too quickly. I looked out the car window at the city skyline and traffic, already missing them. What would greet me in Kingston? It couldn't be anything like this.

She chuckled. "Nice try, Keira, but you're going. She specifically asked for you." She flipped on her turn signal and entered the merge lane heading to the airport.

"But what's she like? Is she going to be a cranky fusspot who's in full blown dementia? God, she's over ninety. What will we talk about?" I could picture it now, me carrying bedpans and watching her drool soup from the corner of her mouth. Gross.

She smiled and glanced over at me. "My mother was...I mean *has* always been one of the smartest women I've ever met. She's sweet but she can be stubborn. I remember once, we were staying at a hotel in Chicago. She took it into her head that she wanted to hear the blues singer playing in a club just down the street. We were late getting there and the place was packed. I wanted to just go back to the room and call it a night. We'd shopped all day and had a big dinner, but she insisted."

"What'd you do?" It was so like Mom to want to crash early and read a book with her feet up.

"The old devil slipped a hundred dollar bill to the bouncer and said she was a friend of the singer, some old Blues legend. Then she turned to me and told me to go back to the hotel." She shook her head and laughed. "She rolled in at around four the next morning. Turned out she *did* know the singer and they partied until all hours."

I couldn't help but laugh. "How old was she then?"

"That was only a few years ago. She was eighty-eight." Her eyebrows rose but there was a small smile on her lips. She leaned forward and peered out the front window looking for the entrance to the parking lot. "You remind me of her in a lot of ways. I'm glad you'll finally get to meet her."

I turned to look out the window, trying to picture what she'd look like. From the sounds of it, she might not be as doughty as I'd originally thought. Which brought me to the question that I hadn't dared to ask. Even *I* had my limits being insensitive. How long would I be banished to the hinterland in

Canada? Until she died?

**

We didn't stop at one of the terminals, instead followed a service road around to where hangars were for smaller companies. Dad had made all the arrangements, chartering a plane to take me directly to the airport in Kingston. We entered the office at the front of one and Mom went to talk to the clerk behind the counter while I wandered over to see what plane I'd be on. I hoped it would be the Lear we took a few times, but if it was a Gulfstream I'd suffer through it. After all, the flight would only take a short while. I had checked on Google and Kingston was less than 300 miles away—an hour and a half tops in a jet.

There was only one plane parked out front and my eyes almost popped out on my cheeks when I saw it. What the hell? It was tiny! No first class champagne flight for me. If you could call it a plane! It looked more like an over-sized mosquito. It not only wasn't a jet, it only had one engine. I could tell because there was only one propeller sticking out the front.

Good grief, the boat Cerise's father had was bigger, and it didn't have to go up in the air!

Some random guy around my age came out of an office behind the counter and shook Mom's hand. She pointed to me at the window and he gave a wave. Uh-oh, from the stripes on the epaulets on his shoulder and the wings pinned to the chest of his blue jacket, I realized this guy was going to be my pilot. He did have a cute smile, but I wanted someone Dad's age to be behind the wheel or whatever you call it in a plane. I wandered over and Mom introduced me to Roy.

"How long have you been a pilot?" I asked.

He chuckled. "Longer than you!"

"Kiera, Roy's licensed on a lot of different aircraft and he's very capable," Mom said, her voice edgy. "Your father specifically requested him." She tilted her head at me. "Do you think for one second that we'd trust your life in the hands of someone with less than a five star rating?"

"Okay, okay!" I said, waving my hands. I looked back at Roy. "You just look... so young."

He gave a smiling sigh. "Don't worry, I get it all the time." Tilting his head towards Mom, he added, "Your mother's right though. I am wicked good." He smiled again. It didn't give me much comfort, but he seemed okay.

Mom bent over and gave me a quick goodbye hug. My eyes started tearing up. Sure, I was taking a chartered plane and the pilot was cute, but I was still basically being kicked out of my home. I hugged back stiffly.

I was still teary eyed from leaving Mom at the gate, but even through the film on my eyes, the plane still looked miniscule; as we approached it, it seemed to get smaller and smaller somehow. He opened the door on the passenger side taking my suitcases, set them into the cramped rear. There were only four seats on this plane, counting the two up front at the controls.

"You'll ride up front with me," Roy said. "It's the most comfortable seat on the plane."

My eyes were saucers as I slipped into the seat and looked around at the instrument panel and gadgets. The pilot and I were going to be shoulder to shoulder.

"This won't take long. We caught a break in the traffic. It looks like we'll be in the air in ten minutes."

To the right of me, in the main section of the airport, large airliners were taxiing down the runway lining up for their take-off. At least it was a clear day with blue skies and hardly any clouds to break the vista. I could be thankful for that at least.

He settled in next to me and placed a set of headphones on his cropped, blonde head. His head jerked from side to side and he closed his eyes. "Roxanne, you don't want to put on the red light." His singing voice was no threat to whatever band had played that tune!

I could only stare, open mouthed when he started to laugh.

"Just kidding. It never gets old for me, seeing the passenger's face when I do that." He started flipping buttons and checking instruments.

"You're hilarious, all right. I hope you can fly this plane better than you sing." I tugged the seat belt over my lap and snapped it shut. *Dad, I'm going to kill you if I don't crash first.*

"Relax. I graduated top of flight training class." Again his grin, the glare from the pearly whites flashing, "Of course, there was only *me* in the class but that doesn't matter, right?"

Seriously? I was about to take my maiden flight in a small plane and a Jerry Seinfeld wannabe was the pilot? Going to see a grandmother I'd never met in some hick town wasn't bad enough? This was a nightmare. I shook my head and looked out the side window again.

"Okaaay. I see this is going to be a loooong flight." He flipped a few more switched and the motor whined to life.

The vibration seemed to go right through me. I'd been on commercial flights before but seeing the propeller twirl so close at the front of the plane made my stomach clench. I clasped my hands so tight together on my lap that the knuckles were ivory.

Beside me, Roy leaned forward and slipped the navy jacket off his shoulders and loosened his tie. There was a small smile on his face and for the first time, he looked professional. We might just make it.

The plane started forward, every crack and dip in the runway registering in my gut. When I looked out the side window, at the wing of the plane, and saw it fluttering, my breath caught in my throat. The wing was so flimsy. Was it gonna fall off?

But surely that was normal. I mean, how many planes actually crashed considering how many were in the air? Not that I would know these statistics, considering the only source of news in my world was Facebook and Google.

He mumbled something into the microphone next to his lips and the plane began to accelerate. I swallowed hard and stared dead ahead, noting the small lights bordering the black tarmac speeding by, faster and faster. I barely dared to breathe as the end of the length of runway closed in. The hum of the tires became softer and then was gone. I looked out and saw the dark surface below me. We were up!

Roy looked over at me and smiled. "There. That wasn't so bad, was it?"

As I was about to answer, the plane rocked on some turbulence and I clutched the arm rests. "We're not there yet." I muttered.

Higher and higher we went until the clouds drifted by like cigarette smoke. Still the plane seemed to be hitting potholes, bumping and bouncing. What happened to the clear, blue sky? This was more like riding waves in a small boat.

The breakfast of sausage and eggs churned in my stomach. My mouth watered and I covered it with my hand, staring wildly at Roy.

He reached down and handed me a wax paper bag. It almost didn't open fast enough before my entire breakfast was deposited inside. My eyes watered and my mouth tasted horrid. When I glanced over at him, he smiled and shook his head.

"Don't worry about that. It happens to the best of us."

I tried swallowing and my free hand dug in my purse for a tissue and gum. I wasn't sure what to do with the soiled and smelly bag. A hot flush crept up my neck. Despite what Roy said, this was embarrassing. "How much longer will this turbulence last?"

"Another three hours, thereabouts." He nodded towards the bag. "You might want to keep that handy." He grinned. "Can you crack the window a little?" Again the chuckle. "Just kidding."

I closed my eyes and sighed. This was going to be an ordeal.

FIVE

I was a wet dish rag stumbling out of the plane three hours later. My knees were limp noodles, and my hair was plastered on my cheeks soaked with sweat. I wasn't sure if undergoing a root canal would be worse than riding in that cramped tin can next to Roy whose joke cracking hadn't let up.

The fresh air felt good on my skin. The sun was still high in the sky, pouring down like honey as I scurried across the tarmac in Kingston.

"This is where I take my leave." Roy nudged me as he set my suitcases on the tiled floor. "The Customs desk is right over there. Good luck to you, Keira."

"Thanks Roy." I managed to make a small smile. "It was a real experience but at least I'm here in one piece."

He put two fingers to his forehead and with a slight nod he saluted me and then sauntered down the corridor. A jaunty whistle of the tune he'd sung just before takeoff followed him. Who the hell was Roxanne?

'CANADA CUSTOMS' emblazoned the high counter just ahead, where a dark suited, middle aged woman sat. When I walked over I handed my passport to her and smiled. She glanced at the photo and eyed me suspiciously comparing the two.

"How long will you be in Canada?" She typed on a keyboard while her eyes flitted to me, daring me to lie.

"I'm here visiting my grandmother who isn't well. So, I'm not sure." Why did I suddenly feel like a criminal, like I was trying to hide something? I hated how these serious bureaucrats could do that to people. Yet if she refused entry into this backwater, would that be so bad?

"Any drugs, alcohol or firearms in your possession?"

I chuckled. What would she do if I said yes? For a moment I was tempted. "No, Ma'am. Left my forty five at home, right next to my stash."

She leaned forward, placing her meaty elbows on the counter. "You do realize I have the power to do a strip search, don't you?"

Oh my God. From the glint in her eye, she'd probably enjoy it! "Sorry. I crack jokes when I'm nervous. Seriously, I haven't anything but my clothes."

She sniffed and lifted her chin. "If you stay any longer than three months, you must check back with Customs." She handed my passport back and turned to her screen, dismissing me.

When I left her station and picked up my bags from the scanning machine, an elderly man who'd been sitting on a bench strode forward. His gaze was steady from an ancient lined face as he extended his hand to take mine.

"Keira?"

I nodded and felt his hand close over mine, noting the dry parchment of his grip.

"I'm Lawrence Brady. Your grandmother sent me to pick you up." He towered over me even though his shoulders were stooped with age. There were laugh lines at the corners of his eyes and his nose was slightly curved, like a hawk's. There was the flash of a smile before he reached and grabbed my suitcase.

"Are you a friend of my grandmother's?" I had to walk fast

to keep up with him as he strode across the terminal. He was lanky and more spry than I would have thought for someone so old.

"I like to think so. I've worked for her for a long time. A very long time." He paused and gestured for me to precede him through the glass doors that slipped open to reveal the warm summer day.

My forehead rose. If he was there looking after her, then why did they need me? "How is she? I mean, I've never met her, but Mom told me she was ill?"

For the first time a genuine smile formed on his lips. "How is your mother?" He stopped at a mammoth black car that even I could tell was a classic. He slid the key into the lock and the back hatch silently rose up.

"She's good. You know her?" I watched him hoist the suitcase and place it gently in the cavern at the rear of the Sherman tank. The sun's ray cast a glint on the lettering above the chrome bumper. 'Cadillac'.

"Know her? I should say so. I practically raised Susie until she went to boarding school." He slammed the lid shut and tossed the keys in the air, catching them swiftly in his gnarled hand. "Let's go."

Susie? I watched him round the car and yank the driver's door open wide before my legs kicked into gear to go to my side of the asphalt yacht. Mom hadn't said anything about this guy, other than to say someone would be there to pick me up at the airport. And yet, he'd raised her?

I climbed into the front seat and sank down into plush leather. I glanced to the side at his profile as he started the engine. He'd evaded my original question, avoiding telling me anything about my grandmother's health. My hand scrambled to the side of the seat searching for my seat belt. Maybe that was part of the code for butlers or whatever he was, that they didn't talk about their employers out of turn.

He pulled out of the parking lot and I turned to gaze out the side window at the sparkling blue lake we skimmed by. I had known that the city would be small after the hustle of New

York but I hadn't expected the quiet vista before me. A few sailboats dotted the expanse of water that the road hugged winding its way along the small curves. We passed by subdivisions of houses and then the outer limits of the city as taller building came into view.

"It's not very far to your grandmother's home. I would give you a tour of the city but I hate to leave her alone for any length of time." He glanced over and his smile was tight. "After New York, Kingston might seem pretty bland. There's a lot of history in this city though. Did you know it was the first capital of Canada?

Did he know I couldn't care less? I just nodded.

The high rise condos on the outskirts gave way to squat limestone and old clapboard homes as we drew closer to the city center.

He pointed at a large domed building. "That's city hall," he said. A grey limestone building spanned the whole block, topped by a pretty cool dome. For a city hall, it looked kind of small, I thought.

He pointed to the opposite side where there was the cutest park and a marina behind it. "And that's Confederation Basin."

"Confederates?" I said. "Were you guys involved in the Civil War?"

He chuckled and just shook his head 'No'.

I stared out the window taking it all in, wondering when the actual city was going to appear. Where were the stores and nightclubs?

I could hardly believe it when we passed over a bridge and the land became greener and buildings sparser. That was it? It seemed more like a small town than a city. I wouldn't be missing much being stuck in the country with my grandmother.

Fifteen minutes later, Lawrence flipped the turn signal on and we drove even slower than the plodding pace he'd maintained since we'd left the airport. A silver mailbox with the name 'York' emblazoned in blue script marked the start of the driveway.

"We're here." Lawrence's eyes lit up and he hunched over the steering wheel, smiling out at the row of trees that bordered the gravel lane.

My stomach clenched tight as I looked ahead at the stately stone structure. The dark grey door perched above a wide set of stone steps, while windows on each side of it and above, formed a line on the second storey. Black shutters framed each window. There was even a row of windows jutting up from the deep slate of the roof. The place was massive for just two people! Surrounding the house was a wooded lot, thick with trees and shrubs of all kinds.

Two Grecian urns filled with a profusion of red flowers and ivy flanked the steps, welcoming me as I stepped from the car. I gulped, looking up at the house. In New York City this home would be behind a wrought iron fence with armed security.

At the sound of the trunk lid banging shut I turned and watched Lawrence, my heavy suitcase stretching his arm as he marched forward. The butterflies in my stomach took flight when I followed him up the steps to the imposing entry.

He pinned me with his steely eyes before turning the gleaming brass handle of the door. "It's just three-thirty. Your grandmother needs to rest at four o'clock. Mind you don't keep her from that schedule. She'll join you at six for a cocktail before dinner, which is at seven, sharp."

My head jerked back and I stared at him. I wasn't even in the door and the orders were being barked at me. "Fine. I'm kind of tired anyway. I could stand a rest myself." It was the truth, and I wasn't letting him have the last word.

Inside the house, I paused looking at the spacious hallway and the wide staircase that curved around to the second floor. The entire foyer was airy, going up to the ceiling on the second floor. A row of golden wood spindles before the expanse of the upstairs gallery gleamed in the light of the chandelier hanging down from the high ceiling above.

At a clatter to my right, I turned and for the first time saw my grandmother. With a hand clasping a black cane with a carved ivory handle, she stood with her chin high; her posture perfect and straight. My eyes opened wide. It was like staring into a mirror, except this version of me was like, a hundred years older! The same dark blue eyes, the nose thin and straight above a mouth that curved up in the corners. But it was her cheekbones that dominated her sculpted face, high and defined even in the soft lines of her skin. She smiled and it was like the sun coming out from behind a cloud.

"Keira." Her hand rose to swipe a tear from her eye. "You are even lovelier in person." Her gait was stiff and slow as she walked towards me.

"Grandmother." My voice was flat. This was the woman who'd never bothered to meet me before this. If she expected me to rush over and gush, she had another think coming.

"Would you like some tea or lemonade, Pamela, before I take Keira's bags up?" Lawrence set the suitcase on the floor and stepped over to her side, placing her hand in the crook of his arm.

The expression in her face as she looked up at him was warm before turning her gaze once more on me. "Keira? Would you care for anything after your long trip?"

"Just a glass of water. Thanks." I was starving and parched but there was no way I was going to ask for anything more.

Grandmother turned back to Lawrence and smiled. "Would you mind bringing a ham and cheese sandwich and a soda for Keira, dear? I'll have a glass of iced tea. We'll have it in the sunroom." She patted his arm and then watched him leave, a smile still playing on her lips." It faded a little when she turned to me. "Come along. I'm looking forward to a chat with you." She winked. "I've waited a long time for that, don't you think?"

She adjusted the high neck of the ruby silk tunic and turned. Her cane tapped lightly on the dark hardwood as she walked past the set of stairs to the back of the house.

I took a deep breath and squared my shoulders before following in her wake. If she had expected me to be all warm and gushing, she was mistaken. In fact, it was more puzzling than ever, why I was even there. Sure she was old but she could get around and she had Lawrence. I stepped up beside her and glanced over, noting the white hair, perfectly coiffed in a loose French roll, the ruby earrings swaying gently against her translucent skin.

"Mom told me you haven't been well, Grandmother." She looked fine to me, even if she moved as slow as a turtle.

"I'm well enough, thanks. " She stepped through the open doorway into a bright room that was a lush jungle. Green plants formed a wall, chest high, while above the sun beamed warmth through the glass dome. In the center of the space were high backed wicker chairs and a small glass table. She eased down into the closest one and sat back.

I took my time, gazing out the glass at an expanse of lawn that flowed down to the lake, where a short dock jutted out. Beds of roses and what looked like a vegetable garden marked the boundary of the property on each side.

"It's gorgeous, isn't it? You don't get this kind of privacy and peace in many places. I've lived all over the world, from Scotland to Singapore." She smiled up at me and her eyes sparkled brightly as she leaned forward and patted the seat next to her. "Sit down and tell me about yourself, dear."

For a moment I was tongue tied. Where would I start? She was a perfect stranger to me, even if she was my grandmother. I took a seat and perched forward, resting my hands on the table. "I'm a Libra. Born October sixth at one twelve in the morning. I like going out partying with my friends and I hate peas."

Her eyes narrowed but she chuckled. "Not to mention you're a total smart ass and that you've tried your hand at social work, photography, and yes...your latest whim was acting."

I sat back and folded my arms over my chest, glaring at her. If this was going to be another lecture—

"You also love animals. Dogs in particular. But they shy away from you when you come near. You always drop coins in a beggar's hand and you have to watch every calorie that you eat. You actually tend to obsess over your hips, truth be told, but you'd rather stick pins in your eyes than exercise." Her eyebrows bobbed. "That rhymes. Pretty good for an old doll, right?"

My mouth fell open. "How do you know these things? Did Mom tell you?" But in truth, the part about giving coins to the homeless was something I never told anyone about. You cancel the karma, if you do that.

"Exactly. When it comes to charity, never let the right hand know what the left is doing. I've done my share of handouts too, Keira." She reached for my hand and pried it from my chest, clasping it tightly.

I was still trying to make sense of her statement. It was as if she read my mind. She held my hand in both of hers, smiling over at me. It was the oddest sensation. My fingers tingled and a sense of calm seeped into my bones.

"You haven't found your calling yet, Keira. That's something I hope will change after you've been here a while." She turned when Lawrence appeared in the doorway, a tray of food and glasses in his spotted hands. He focused on my grandmother holding my hand and the smile on his lips vanished.

Grandmother sat back and patted my wrist before her hands dropped to the table. "Thank you, dear. What would I do without you dear Lawrence?" She smiled up at him as he set the sandwich and glasses down.

When he left, I took the linen napkin and spread it on my lap. "Which brings me to the question, Grandmother..." I looked over at her. "Why am I here? You have Lawrence and to be honest, you look pretty healthy. Mom and Dad made it sound like you were dying or something."

She took a sip of her iced tea and then set it down softly. "What you really want to know is why this is the first time, you've ever met me. Isn't that so?"

I nodded and then bit into the sandwich, waiting for her answer. Once more, she'd hit the nail right on the head. It hadn't been a money issue, since she was obviously doing pretty well.

"It's the same reason I sent your mother away to attend boarding school when she was nine. The nature of my work..." She looked down at her drink for a few moments. "Let's just say, that it was for her protection and with you... the need was even greater." Her eyes were soft gazing at me. "I was there the day you were born. I held you and I knew right away how special you really are."

"I don't understand. Protection from who? And why? Who were you protecting me from?" I pushed the plate containing the other part of my sandwich away. Suddenly, my appetite was gone. Either she was making this up...the delusions of an old woman or everything was a sham. Growing up in New York, my life had been pretty normal. Loving parents, a nice home, school. And this woman was making it sound like I was in the witness protection program.

She had to be senile. But what about Mom? She'd sent her away to boarding school and for sure Grandmother had been a lot younger. Maybe she was some kind of paranoid schizophrenic.

"Let me assure you I'm totally sane." She got up and wandered over to the wall of tropical plants, plucking dead leaves away and straightening the arrangement. Her face was set and she took a deep breath. "You'll just have to trust me on this, Keira. It's a lot to take in and I don't want to overwhelm you with detail."

"But Grandmother! You uprooted me from my home! You owe me some kind of an explanation!" I clasped the sides of the chair, trying to keep from jumping up and shaking her! This was so unfair to be banished to another country with some bullshit story about protecting me.

"And you will get that explanation...in time." She wandered over and her fingers stroked my cheek as she gazed down at me. "Such a feisty girl. That's good. But Keira, I wish you'd call me Nana. Grandmother sounds so formal and cold. I want us to be close."

I huffed a sigh. There was nothing worse than having to wait...being treated like a child. It was a hook to keep me there.

I just knew it. And I'd be damned if I was going to call her Nana. This whole situation was so manipulative. I forced a small smile. "You don't like Grandmother? How about GM, instead? It's less formal and much more appropriate than 'Nana'. As you said, we need to get to know each other before you've earned that title."

Her face broke into a wide grin and the crow's feet at her eyes became deeper. "It's a deal." Her hand went to the wispy hair at the back of her head and she fluffed it, preening as she took a seat again. "I kind of like that. "GM. It'll work."

Whatever. I craned my neck, gazing around at my surroundings. "This is a pretty posh place for just you and that Lawrence guy."

She looked at me evenly. "It's paid for. As is the trust fund that has supported your family all your life—well before you were born, I might add."

She answered the question before I had it completely formulated in my head. This old gal was pretty quick witted, that was for sure. "So GM, how did you make so much money?" I pulled the plate back, deciding to finish the sandwich. My stomach was growling and Lawrence made a mean ham and cheese.

"I played the stock market. It was like taking candy from a baby. Then I travelled the world, meeting royalty and the elites in all the major centers." She bobbed her eyes at me. "Jet setters and A-listers. I didn't do too bad for a kid from Oklahoma, raised on a farm." She snorted and laughed. "You think you like to party? Keira, I've done it all!"

Lawrence appeared in the doorway and pointed at the gold wrist watch on his arm. His gaze centered on my grandmother.

"All right. I know, it's time." She turned to me and smiled. "Make yourself at home. Lawrence will show you around after he tucks me in. You'll want the internet password and such." She got to her feet and ambled over to take his arm. "I've arranged for you to move into the top floor. It's actually a self contained apartment although I expect you to have dinner with me at seven each night. I'm eager for us to get to know each other."

With that she left, leaving a scent of roses in her wake. It was at that moment that the sun disappeared behind a grey cloud and raindrops splattered the glass dome above me. I looked over at a plant nestled in the dark green foliage; a white cusp shaped flower. It was familiar, yet odd.

When I went to get up, a wave of dizziness washed through me and I sunk down once more. Looking around at the mini greenhouse with the rain streaking the glass, the oddest sensation filled my very core. I'd been here before. Even the crust of the sandwich on the plate...I'd already experienced all of this, from the rain pelting the glass to the lushness of the foliage, the air warm and humid, with a sweet earthy smell.

But that couldn't be! I'd never ever been in a solarium like this, surrounded by tropical plants. Yet, I knew in my bones that I had! Was this a deja vu experience? I'd read about it but this was the first I'd ever experienced it. As well as making my knees turn to rubber, it was disorienting.

SIX

I decided to stay put until Lawrence returned. Even though GM had said to make myself at home, it was still weird to be there. She was my grandmother, my own flesh and blood yet she was a stranger and this was her turf.

The fact that when she'd left, I'd had that spell of déjà vu wasn't lost on me either. It had been a day. From getting up early to that white knuckled flight and throwing up almost the whole way...it was probably normal to feel disoriented. Hell, I was even in a foreign country! I finished the Coke and closed my eyes, taking deep breaths.

One thing that hadn't come up in the conversation with my grandmother was how long she expected me to stay there. It was too long a way to come for a short visit and my parents had made it abundantly clear that there was no place in their home for me anymore. And the fact that GM had an apartment set up in her home...well, that didn't bode well for a quick visit either.

Plus what was all this talk about protection? Mom and Dad had never once tried to shelter me from going where I wanted or doing anything I chose. Surely, if they had felt threatened they would have limited me a bit more? None of this made much sense. Yet, GM was a sharp old lady. If I didn't know any better, there'd been times that I could have sworn she was reading my mind.

"Keira?"

I jumped in my seat and my eyes flew open. Lawrence stood across from me, reaching for the empty glasses. There was a glint in his eyes. "Are you ready for me to show you the rest of the house, specifically your quarters?"

"Yes." I and tossed the napkin onto the table. "The sandwich was good. Thanks."

"Would you mind bringing your plate? We might as well start with the kitchen."

My eyes flashed to his and I paused for a beat. At home, I wouldn't have thought anything of clearing my dishes away but we didn't have a butler or whatever it was that Lawrence did. It was clear that he worked for GM but his butler service didn't extend to me. "Sure." I forced a casual smile and picked up the napkin and plate. If he was trying to get under my skin, I wasn't going to show him it was working.

I followed him from the room and through the corridor under the main set of stairs. He veered to the right and pushed a door open with his shoulder. When I entered the kitchen it was a total surprise. Even though the house was an antique with high ceilings and dark wooden baseboards that were almost a foot high, this room was the height of modern living with stainless steel appliances and polished granite countertops. A small table was placed at the far end beside a spacious window that showed a view of the garden and river.

Lawrence folded his body over the open door of the dishwasher and set the glasses inside. "It's too bad the rain started. I could have shown you the river and the gardens. Pamela's roses are as beautiful as any horticulturalist's." He smiled and his gaze at me softened. "Roses are her favourite flower."

"Does she tend to them herself?" It seemed odd that she

would, considering she used a cane when she walked.

His eyebrows rose high and he chuckled. "She oversees! No, I do most everything around here." He pulled back as if seeing me for the first time. "I suppose, I should ask if you have any food allergies. It wouldn't do to serve you mushrooms if you swell up like a balloon."

"Nope. Although I'm not overly fond of pork, I love bacon, though I try to limit it." It would probably be a stretch to hope for marshmallows and melon.

He plucked the plate from my hand and slid it into the dishwasher. "No worries about meals then. I serve dinner and anything else that Pamela wants...but for breakfast and lunch, you're on your own. I assume that you'll manage. Make a list of any foods you want and I'll see that they're delivered. We're kind of light on frozen pizza and we're too far from town for take-out."

His eyebrows bobbed high and a small grin formed on his lips. "We'll start with the dining room." He led the way through another door and we entered a large room with a table that could have easily sat a regiment. A crystal chandelier hung low over the center, and lining the closest wall was a large dark cabinet. A vase of red roses that were starting to wilt topped a linen cloth, and a decanter of brandy sat next to it.

"Can I include wine and gin on the list of items I would like?"

"Just add it to the list."

"And melon? Honeydew if you can get it. And marshmallows. Not the mini's either—the biggest ones you can find."

He gave me that look I've seen a million times. I get that look whenever anyone asks me what my favorite snack food is and I tell them the truth. Honeydew melon and big marshmallows. You can keep your ice cream, pretzels or whatever; that's mine. So, needless to say, Lawrence stared at me like I was out of my mind.

He gave his head a slight shake. "You did say marshmallows and melon, right?"

"Yep. Can't get enough of it. Big marshmallows."

"Ohhkaaay. Just put it on the list."

Nodding, I continued perusing the dining room. I paused to look at the large oil canvas displayed on the far wall. There was something forlorn about it. A young woman with long auburn locks in an old fashioned white robe perched on the seat of a rowboat. Weeds and bull rushes scraped the hull of the boat that was sitting near the shore, the water a marine blue. The dappled sunlight from overhead highlighted the folds of her dress and the tapestry casually draped over the side of the boat. But it was her look of longing, gazing off in the distance that made me stare.

"A curse is on her, if she stay." Lawrence had sidled up beside me, gazing at the painting. "It's an original Waterhouse in his Lady of Shalott series. Perhaps you read the poem in school. The painting was a rare find for Pamela when she was in England." He turned and opened the door at the far end of the room.

"Thanks." I slipped by him and was once more in the airy foyer of the house. The gloom of the day outside had settled and now the high corners were shadowed and the balustrade above on the second floor looked more like the bars of a prison.

His footsteps were soft crossing the floor and he paused in the arched opening. "The living room." His hand made a sweep inviting me to take a peek inside.

As miffed as I was being banished to this house, I have to admit it was a gorgeous room. From the prim French Provincial style of the sofa and chairs, clad in a floral upholstery to the stone fireplace at the far end. The windows showed rivulets of rain behind the lacy curtains and a cushion covered the deep wells of the sill. It would be a great place to sit and read a book or surf the web with a computer passing the time.

Lawrence cleared his throat, signalling that this part of the tour had ended. I joined him again and as we passed the next closed door, his voice lowered. "That's the library but it's been converted to a bedroom for Pamela. She doesn't do stairs anymore. The cane helps with the rheumatism in her hips, but climbing stairs has become too much for her."

He started up the wide arc of the circular staircase and turned to me. "My room is on the second floor as well as two other bedrooms and a bathroom. There're laundry facilities in a small alcove next to the bathroom." He wasn't even winded from the hike up the stairs, whereas I was feeling the strain in my legs. "Any questions?"

I stepped up onto the second floor landing, and paused looking down the hallway. A series of closed doors, and an oriental runner covering the center of the hardwood floors before them, met my eye. The half moon window at the end of the hallway broke the expanse of the wall, the dull light from the outside peeking through. "This place is huge. Do you ever have guests or is this just empty space?"

"Very rarely, but it has happened a few times." His head jerked to the side. "My room and bath is over there."

As we climbed the final narrower set of stairs, I remembered my computer. "We have internet, right? What's the password to log on?" If I was to stay sane in this house, I'd need to connect to the outside world. Plus, I probably should send an email to my parents to let them know I survived the trip. Mom had some hard questions coming her way with all this talk of protection.

He snorted. "Susie Q. Capital 'S' and 'Q'." He glanced over at me and rolled his eyes. "There was a popular song way back when and besides it's your mother's name. I'll write it out for you." He reached over and swung open the door to what was going to be my room.

I ignored the subtle put down because my eyes widened when my bed sitting room appeared. It had to be almost thirty feet long with ceilings that sloped down to side walls that were only a few feet high. There were windows cut into the roof, casting light over the golden hardwood floors. A queen sized bed with the same comforter I'd had in my apartment sat against the far wall. Even my Mexican rug was there!

I raced past my luggage and sat on the bed, testing it for softness. It was perfect. A desk, a small sofa and chair in the center of the room as well as a small counter with a sink, a fridge and microwave perched on the other side of the room. If it wasn't stuck in the middle of nowhere, the apartment would be great.

"There are cupboards in the knee walls for more storage." Lawrence wandered over to a section between the two windows and a recessed door slid back, revealing drawers with antique brass handles. He straightened and closed the sliding door once more. "You'll find fresh fruit, soda, milk and cheese in the fridge and a supply of cookies and coffee in the cabinets."

He wandered over to the kitchen and took a notebook and pen from his shirt pocket. "Here's the password for the internet." He paused and sighed. "Your bathroom is just over there, on the other side of these stairs. If you need anything else, just let me know. Your grandmother will be up at six for cocktails in the living room." He nodded and disappeared down the stairs.

Now that I was alone in my new quarters, I decided to explore. I walked by the stairwell and opened the door to my bathroom. Against one wall, was an over sized, high, antique claw bathtub, while the sink and vanity claimed the opposite side, next to the toilet. The place was huge with black and white ceramic tile, and walls painted an oyster shell pink.

I couldn't help but realize that G. M. had laid everything out just for me. Mom and Dad must have sent my comforter and apartment items ahead to make the place seem more like home. All in all, it was exactly how I would have decorated it.

I plucked my cell phone from my pocket to check the time. It was a twenty past four. The long day was wearing on my bones and I'd have just enough time to take a nap before I had to meet GM. My shoulders sagged as I wandered out of the bathroom and back into the bedroom area.

I stopped short when I saw my bed. The comforter was now folded back, showing a triangle of crisp white sheets below the pillow. My gaze shot to the stairwell for any sign of Lawrence. But it was empty. That guy moves like a cat. Who else would have turned down the bed for me? GM was asleep and besides she didn't do stairs.

Another wave of dizziness flooded through me and I reached for the side of the sofa to steady myself as I continued to stare at the bed. My stomach churned and the sandwich that had tasted so good earlier, was now sour, gurgling up my throat. I took a few deep breaths to settle it down and swallowed hard.

The bed that had seemed so inviting before, held little appeal now. Someone had been in my room, invading my privacy. There must be another person working there. It was the only explanation and the more I thought about it, the more sense it made, considering that Lawrence was so old. There was no way he'd be able to cook, care for G.M and maintain the housekeeping. It would have been nice if he'd introduced the other staff though, instead of them creeping me out like this.

Either he did it, or had instructed someone else do this without telling me. At any rate, I wasn't so sure that he liked me being there.

SEVEN

I shook off the dizzy spell and decided to use the time before meeting up with GM to unpack and settle into my room. There was even time to spare to send off an email to Mom and Dad. I couldn't wait to see what they came back with about this 'protection' business.

It had been a few days since I let my friends know via email and some Snapchats that I was kicked out of school and lost my apartment. None of them—not even Cerise—had bothered to reply. Not a peep, and some of these guys I grew up with! I was tempted to phone Cerise and give her a piece of my mind. But really, why bother? So after shooting off my email to my parents I closed my laptop. I stared at it for a minute and then put it back into its travel case and tucked it beside the desk. Maybe going off grid for a while was a good idea anyway.

I looked at the clock and saw that GM would be 'expecting' me for cocktails before dinner shortly. I stood up to start getting ready.

In the bathroom, I stared at my reflection wondering if I

was supposed to change into something more formal for dinner with GM. It probably wouldn't hurt. I'd been sick in the plane and the shirt and jeans seemed pretty stale from that experience. I turned the shower on, before peeling the layers of clothes off and leaving them in a tussled heap in the center of the floor.

Even the shampoo and body wash set out for me were ones that I used back home. GM had gone to a lot of trouble to make me feel welcome. The hot water was wonderful on my skin and I hummed a tune as I lathered the perfumed soap into my skin. After a few minutes the pressure dropped and the water cooled. Just my luck that Lawrence would pick this time of day to run the dishwasher or laundry, hogging the hot water.

I turned the water off and reached for the towel hanging on the bar next to the tub. It was fluffy and soft on my skin when I dried off and then stepped out, pondering what to wear. I could probably get away with leggings and my long silk top with the gold earrings and bangles.

I reached for my terry robe hanging behind the door and my gaze drifted to the floor. My clothes. There was no sign of my jeans or the top I'd been wearing. My eyes opened wide and I tugged the sides of the robe tight to my chin. How dare they! Someone had come in, unannounced while I was naked in the shower and taken my clothes!

I ran the comb through my hair, tugging a few stray strands out in the process. A small spot in the mirror appeared from the cloud of condensation and my nostrils flared as I yanked at my hair. This was too much! I'd have to speak to GM about this! If this was my space then whatever servant was creeping around up here, cleaning up and setting my comforter back had better buzz off. I hated people touching my stuff, on a good day; the idea of people I didn't even know going through my things really, really pissed me off.

Grabbing my make-up case, I sneered wondering if it had been rifled as well. I smeared some lipstick on and freshened my mascara. It was my grandmother's eyes that stared back at me—the same, shade of blue and the slight upward tilt at the corners. Well, she might be trying her best to make me into a mini-me of her but I was having none of it. At least I respected other people's privacy, dammit.

My footsteps slapped the floor as I strode into the bedroom. Spying the wicker clothes hamper, I stomped over and lifted the lid. Yup. The clothes I'd been wearing earlier, lay in a tangled heap. If I hadn't needed to wash them before, I definitely needed to do that now. Someone's hands had been all over them.

***

When I stepped into the living room, GM was already perched on the sofa. Her eyes were crinkled in a smile above the choker neckline of the white dress draping her frail frame. The jewel of her tennis bracelet caught the light when she lifted her frosted glass of a pale drink. The only sign that she'd been sleeping earlier was the fact that a few wisps of hair now escaped the loose roll at the back of her head.

"Keira. Would you care for a gin gimlet? Lawrence has made a pitcher of them." She gestured to a sideboard tucked in an alcove near the window. "I hope you found your room comfortable and that you have everything that you need."

Gin gimlet, huh? My favorite drink when I go out with Cerise just happened to be the cocktail for this evening?

She gave me a quick smile. "I adore a nice gin gimlet in the evening; it's my favorite cocktail."

"I'll bet it is," I said as I ambled over to the table to fill a glass that had been left for me.

"So, do you like your room?"

"Everything is great!" I picked up the glass and turned to join her on the sofa. "The only thing...well, I'm a private person and I'm used to doing things for myself. I don't need your maid to turn down my bed or pick up after me." In an annoyed tone I added, "I don't like people touching me, GM, and the idea of people I don't know touching my clothes kind of grosses me out, okay?"

Her eyebrows rose and she smiled. "We don't have a maid, Keira. There are a couple of women who come in twice a week to clean and dust but other than that, it's just Lawrence and me."

"Come on! My clothes...someone picked them up from the bathroom floor and deposited them into the hamper. And my comforter..." I knew Lawrence had gone downstairs before that had happened but I couldn't be sure about the clothes. But wait...the water pressure in the shower had dropped like he'd been using an appliance somewhere else in the house.

GM took a sip of the drink, eyeing me above the rim of the glass. "Lawrence has prepared roast beef with Yorkshire pudding for dinner tonight. It's one of my favourites...in honour of you being here."

"So there's no one else here but the three of us?" I wasn't letting go of this just yet.

She chuckled and patted my knee. "Not a living soul, my dear."

Ha! Not a soul that she knew of. She sounded totally sincere. Yet, how could she be so blasé about this after all the talk earlier about protecting me? The house was in the middle of nowhere and Lawrence hadn't used a key to enter when we arrived from the airport. They probably never locked their doors. They'd get eaten alive in the Big Apple.

"GM," I looked down at my lap for a moment. "Someone moved my clothes from the bathroom, and it wasn't Lawrence, you or me. I think someone has broken into your house." Even as I said it, the absurdity of the situation made my neck get warm. A burglar who tidied up? That didn't make any sense.

"I could save serious money on housekeeping if people broke in and cleaned houses." The smile dropped from her lips and she leaned closer. "How did you feel when that happened?"

My head jerked back and I stared at her. What an odd question. "I was angry of course. I don't like people pawing through my stuff!"

"That's all?" She looked down at the drink in her hand. "You didn't smell anything or feel a little off kilter?" Her dark eyes rose to meet mine.

I huffed a fast sigh. Someone was in the house and she was acting like some kind of therapist? Asking about my feelings?

My forehead tightened. I had clutched the side of the sofa because of the dizziness when I saw the coverlet of the bed pulled back. Was this what she meant? "Actually, I did feel a little nausea." I leaned away from her and my grip on the glass became tighter. "GM what's going on?"

At the series of taps, I turned and saw Lawrence standing in the archway, his gaze gentle as he watched my grandmother. "Anytime you're ready, Pamela? Dinner is warm in the oven if you'd like another drink with Keira."

"Thank you, dear. I'll just finish this one and I'll be ready. Another ten minutes?"

He turned to me. "How's your drink? Would you like me to make another for you?"

Lawrence had made me the sandwich earlier and served the soda. Had he put anything in it that would have made me dizzy? Since I arrived, I'd had two spells of it, something that had never happened before. "Don't go to any trouble. If I want another, I'll make it, Lawrence. Thanks anyway."

I watched him nod and then disappear soundlessly across the foyer. "He's been with you a long time, hasn't he? I mean, he told me he practically raised my mother." My eyes searched her face.

She nodded, making the diamond drop earrings sparkle in the low light. "It seems like forever. I was staying in the Ritz. Your mother was only two at the time. He was working as a waiter there, delivering room service for Susan and the Nanny I'd hired to look after her. I was out visiting friends but when I returned that night, Lawrence was there, in the room reading a bed time story to Susan."

"What? Where was the Nanny?"

"She was out cold. She'd been drinking and actually staggered when he brought the food up. He didn't feel right leaving Susan in her care. It's a good thing he stayed because it wasn't long after, that the old fool actually passed out." She took a deep breath and smiled. "I hired him on the spot, seeing his concern for my little girl. We've been together ever since."

GM was rich; she admitted as much to me. It showed from the house and furnishings to the very clothes on her back. Maybe Lawrence had seen an opportunity back then to get close to my grandmother. It was his word that the Nanny had been drunk. What if he poisoned her to take her place and ever since he'd been ingratiating himself to GM to live the high life? GM had to be at least ten years older than him and maybe he was now eyeing his inheritance.

Before I arrived that is.

"Does he eat with us?" Surely he wouldn't doctor the food if he had to eat it as well.

"Usually we eat together but he won't while you're here. He wants to give us a chance to visit. He's thoughtful that way. He was like a father to Susan." She sighed and her gaze drifted to the window, where the fading light cast a glow.

"So who is my grandfather? Whatever happened to him?" Now that I'd met my grandmother, I was curious to know more.

"I don't know." She smiled and her eyebrows bobbed high.

"You don't know where he is..." I shook my head and leaned closer. "...or you don't know who my mother's father is."

"Both, I'm afraid." She smiled and some colour came into her cheeks. "You must think I'm awful to admit that, but it's the truth. For years, I was the party girl. I had a series of relationships." She chuckled. "Is it a series when they're concurrent? Let's just say that your grandfather was a kind man. They were all kind and devilishly handsome."

She set the unfinished drink on the coffee table and then her hands closed over the cane, pulling herself to her feet. A smile lit her face when she looked down at me. "You'd never know it now, but at one time I was the belle of the ball. Dancing till dawn and sharp as a tack the next day."

For just a moment the old flame sparked in her face and I had no trouble believing what she'd said. Even though lines etched her skin, her eyes and the bones in her face showed classic beauty. She'd been such a hot commodity that she didn't even know who the father of her only child was. To be shocked would be hypocritical. I'd had my share of guys as well. Luckily, birth control had advanced since my grandmother's time.

I swallowed the rest of my drink and stood up, extending my elbow to her. "You are a card GM. How did Mom ever turn out so conservative? None of those guys you were with were like that?"

She squeezed my arm before her hand rested gently there. "If they were, I wouldn't have been with them very long. No, it had to be some recessive quirk in the gene pool."

I laughed and we entered the dining room, arm and arm— two peas in a pod. Yeah, I was warming up to the old doll.

***

The table was set with fine china and a candelabra that cast flickering warmth over the fresh bouquet of red roses. I watched Lawrence stand at the side board slicing the beef that held a tinge of pink in the center. Bowls of steaming oven roasted potatoes, Harvard beets and the Yorkshire puddings were lined up before me. If Lawrence was trying to poison me, it wouldn't be with this meal, not when GM would be sharing the food. There was a genuine affection between the two of them.

"Bon appetite!" Lawrence set the platter of meat next to my grandmother and then with a smile, he left us to our dinner.

"Dig in, Keira. Lawrence is an excellent cook." She helped herself to the beef and then slathered it with gravy. "Is there anyone special in your life, Keira? Some guy that stands out?"

"No one in particular. I went out with a guy for a year but it kind of fizzled and died. We parted friends and I still follow him on Facebook." I took the platter of meat from her hand

and put two thick slices onto my plate.

"All this social media! In my day, we really did socialize and the media was there to take pictures. Oh the glamour of the dresses and movie stars. DeNiro and Redford were crazy card sharks, did you know that?" She smiled and her eyes closed for a moment, reliving the time.

"They're not my grandfather then. Not from the sounds of it."

THUD!

I jumped in my seat and spun around to see what had caused the bang. A picture, a small one displaying a vase spilling over with yellow roses, had fallen to the floor.

Lawrence burst through the door and his eyes examined GM He shot a dark look my way before he spotted the picture on the floor. "Again?" he said.

"I'm afraid so."

As he stepped over to where the painting lay, he muttered, "That Jarrod!"

"Lawrence!" GM snapped.

"Oh, sorry." He glanced over at me. "I'm upset with... the handyman we use is all..." his voice faded. I could tell he was lying through his teeth, but held my tongue. He picked the picture up, feeling the back of it and holding a thin wire between his fingers. He glanced at G.M and sighed. "Sorry. The wire snapped."

The glow of the candles cast dark shadows under my grandmother's eyes when she set her knife and fork on the plate before her. She took a ragged breath and her eyes were hard staring at him. "Tomorrow, please check the other painting. I don't want my Waterhouse damaged."

"Of course, Pamela." He took the painting with him when he walked back through to the kitchen.

The mood in the room turned solemn. GM sat back and lifted the napkin from her lap, depositing it next to her plate. She looked tired and drawn from the surprise of the picture falling, the frailty of her years showing in the lines of her face. "You'll have to excuse me, Keira. I'm afraid I didn't sleep well earlier and I'm exhausted. Please finish your dinner and don't worry about me." She rose to her feet, holding the edge of the table in her hands. Her skin was mottled and parchment thin, showing a map of blue tinged veins.

She tapped the cane on the floor and immediately, Lawrence appeared, pushing the door wide. The expression on his face was tight and worried. "Pamela?"

"I'm ready, Lawrence. Please take me to my room and then see that Keira has everything she needs."

My stomach was a knot as I watched them toddle across the room and then go through the door. The picture falling had really shaken GM up. But, considering her age, any sort of shock would probably do that. But she wasn't the only one. A pall had settled in the dining room and the flames of the candles faltered, casting shadows in the corners of the room. The hair on the back of my neck tingled and I turned to examine behind me. I felt eyes peering at me but there was nothing there. Nothing but the painting of the Lady of Shalott.

The room felt like it was closing in. I rose and picked up the two plates, pushing my way into the kitchen. The gleaming aluminum refrigerator purred quietly and the overhead lights were bright and steady. A plate of food sat untouched on the table below the window. I breathed a sigh of relief, only then aware that I'd been holding my breath.

The feeling of being watched evaporated in the glare of the modern kitchen. I finished scraping the plates and loading them into the dishwasher. There were still items in the dining room but for some reason the thought of going back there totally creeped me out.

Lawrence could get them later. It had been a long day and I was tired. The strain of meeting my grandmother was wearing me down. I'd feel better in the morning after a good night's sleep.

EIGHT

I got out of my clothes and hung them in the small closet set next to the bed. I tossed my underclothes in the hamper and grabbed a cotton nightgown from the chest of drawers. There was no way I was taking any chances leaving clothes lying around. The comforter was still pulled back and I clambered into it, pulling it up to my chin.

When I reached to turn the bedside lamp off, I was in complete, silent blackness. No street lights filtered into the room and no cars and busses rushed by. I was in the country, in the middle of nowhere. I'd never experienced anything as still or dark as this. I might have a hard time drifting off to sleep with all this peace and quiet.

I turned the light back on and got out of bed. Crossing the room to the kitchenette, I flipped the florescent light under the cabinet to life. It lit the green countertop but the glow didn't extend much beyond the loveseat and chair. Just enough light to be familiar for me to sleep with. With a resigned, yet thankful shrug of my shoulders, I retrieved my laptop. So much for being off the grid. I surfed till I found a site that featured street noise, with muted car horns and the sound of traffic. I left it on my desk with the speakers turned low and the screen off.

When I started back to the bed the sound of water hissing through a tap filled my ears. I peered at the computer and then turned to look down the hallway where the bathroom was. A light showed under the door, spreading out across the hardwood. I froze in place, my heart leaping to my throat. There was someone in my bathroom! Probably that same person who had taken my clothes and arranged the bed for me!

I looked around for a weapon. Something to defend myself in case whoever it was, was dangerous. I had a feeling it was a woman, not some burly thug. Why else would they pick up my laundry?

The kitchen! I rushed over and yanked a drawer out, Good! There were knives lined up there. I grabbed the biggest one and tiptoed down the hall. Stopping just outside the door, the sound of water pouring from the tap was louder now. But other than that, there was nothing else.

Quick as a flash, my hand gripped the door handle and I burst inside. My eyes took in all of the room in one sweep and my jaw fell open. The only sign of life was the water hissing from the tap and spiralling down the drain. I stepped over to the tub and peeked behind the shower curtain. Again, nothing. My shoulders drooped and a sigh of relief passed my lips. I stood for a moment, willing my heart to slow, my hand gradually loosening its grip on the wooden handle of the knife.

But if there wasn't anyone there, how had the tap turned on? I reached out and pushed the porcelain lever shut. The sounds of hydraulic air brakes drifted in from the other room, making me jerk to the side. It was the computer. The white noise I had selected. God, I was jumpy as a cat.

But the water running in the sink was weird. I had used the bathroom when I came up but I know I had turned the tap off as well as the light. Yet, the only person up here was me. There was no way anyone could have got by me after I turned the light on. And it hadn't happened until I had used my computer.

My grandmother's words rang in my ear as if hearing them for the first time. 'Not a living soul.' I looked into the mirror, feeling the blood drain from my face as the full impact of her words sank in. The key word had been 'living'. The whites of my eyes rimmed the blue orbs and I gasped.

The place was haunted? Of course I'd seen my share of horror movies, being more scared than I'd ever want to admit to. But I'd never expected to actually be in one!

Even more sinister was the fact that grandmother in all likelihood, knew that when she'd asked me here. What the hell? She didn't have the decency to maybe inform me of that fact when I'd told her about the clothes and the bed thing!

No wonder she'd gotten so shaken up with the picture falling from the wall. She knew it was some kind of ghost thing...and so did Lawrence! The two of them conniving together...

Hell, now I knew why she'd been so calm when I told her my clothes had been moved. And her question, asking me how I felt when that happened. She was fishing to see if I'd clued in that her house was haunted.

For two cents, I'd go down there and wake her up. She'd get a piece of my mind before I called a cab and high-tailed it out of there!

"Argh!" I had no money nor credit cards!

I rushed out of the room and down the hall, grabbing my cell phone from its charger on the kitchen counter. I punched my mother's contact number and then held the small phone firmly to my ear. After a few seconds of dead air, I looked at the screen. 'No service detected.' Great! Now the cell service was down and I was stuck here!

The deadly silence in the room caught my attention. The sounds of traffic that had filled the air earlier was gone. I slammed the phone onto the counter and stormed over to the laptop sitting on the small coffee table. The screen was black and not a light showed in the crease of the gadget. I couldn't even send her an email!

I stomped over to the fridge and yanked the door open wide. Through the clear plastic of the vegetable tray, I spied the melon. I pulled the tray out and my fingers closed over the plump fruit. Nudging the fridge door shut with my hip, I turned to the cabinets. Somehow, I just knew there'd be marshmallows.

After the dinner had been short circuited, I was starving! If I had to bunk in a haunted house, at least I'd gorge on my favourite comfort food. It would be a long time before I'd be able to fall asleep.

I sliced the fruit and dug out the seeds, leaving them in a pulpy mush on the counter. Grabbing a plate and the bag of marshmallows, I headed to the bed. It was stationed against the wall providing a good view of the long room and hallway. If there were any ghosts hanging around, I'd see them coming.

NINE

I woke with a start. Sunlight streamed through the windows, and I looked around cautiously, my cheek snuggled into the pillow. The sofa and chair were exactly as I'd left them and the laptop was on the coffee table. I pushed myself up and peered over at the kitchen.

The green countertop was shiny and clean. "Hmph!" The melon seeds I'd scooped out were nowhere to be seen. Whatever this was, hanging around the old house was obsessed with order. Probably I'd left a trace of toothpaste in the sink when I'd brushed my teeth before bed and that was why the water had been turned on. It had still been kind of creepy.

I threw the covers back and swung my legs over the side of the bed, feeling the solid coolness of the floor under my feet. I had thought that I'd be awake all night, keeping vigil, but I'd slept like a baby. Actually, it was the best sleep I'd had in a long time. Still, I was going to have a few words with my grandmother about all this.

When I passed by the stairwell I paused, listening for any sounds below. The sun was well above the horizon and it had to be close to eleven. Oh well. It wasn't like I had to get up for school anymore. Actually, aside from cocktails and dinner with GM my time was pretty much my own. I still didn't get why she needed me here...not with Lawrence taking care of her. And the fact that the room was seriously spooky wasn't helping her case.

I yawned as I ambled down the hall and into the bathroom. After turning the shower on, I shimmied out of the nightgown and let it fall to the floor. I looked down at it and my eyes narrowed, wondering if the ghost would put it away for me. When I stepped into the tub and felt the water pour down on my head, I smiled.

"Put that away for me, will you Molly?" Molly. The name had popped into my head and seemed just perfect. Molly the Maid. As I rubbed shampoo into my hair, I pictured her, the navy dress with the starched, white lace collar. I mean, if I had to put up with a ghost, at least she was a useful one...so far.

"Do you do laundry, Molly? That'd be nice."

The door slammed shut and I jumped out of my skin. I swiped the soap from my face and peeked out the curtain. The nightgown was gone. There was no doubt who picked it up but she sure didn't have a sense of humour. I smiled when the water cascaded over my head, rinsing the shampoo away. I guess laundry was a stretch for her. I'd better not push my luck.

I don't know why, but in the daytime, ghosts weren't nearly as scary.

After finishing in the bathroom, taking the time to blow dry my hair and force some sort of order to my red tinted curls, I wandered back into the bedroom. The bed was still a disheveled heap of sheets and comforter. I could leave it. Maybe by the time I came back after spending the day exploring the outside, it would be made up—just like in a hotel but without the need to tip.

I chose a blue T shirt and jean shorts and quickly got dressed. My stomach growled in agreement when I slipped a pair of sandals on and headed downstairs. Lawrence stood at the bottom set of steps, a glass of iced tea in his hand.

"Your grandmother is in the solarium." His eyes travelled down my bare legs and his eyebrows drew together. "I take it you're going to explore the grounds today? Perhaps you'd be kind enough to take your grandmother along. She likes to get out to see her roses when the weather is good."

"Tell her, I'll join her in a few. I'd like to grab a bowl of cereal and make a coffee." I was about to step away to go to the kitchen when his voice stopped me cold.

"How did you sleep?"

His eyes bore into mine, searching for any sign of hesitancy.

"Fine, all things considered." I strode across the foyer and pushed the kitchen door wide. Let him chew on that! There was no way I was letting him know what I'd discovered. If he was trying to get under my skin, I wasn't going to give him the satisfaction.

I helped myself to the corn flakes and smiled seeing the almost full pot of coffee. There wasn't an item out of place on the counter or table and it was obvious that they'd been up for hours. Still, it was nice to have coffee still there.

When I stepped out into the bright sunroom, my grandmother sat regally in the high backed chair, the collar of her white cotton blouse extended up above a red paisley scarf. Her hair that yesterday had been upswept showed many loose tendrils draping over her shoulders. Even her make-up couldn't hide the dark circles under her eyes and the lines in her face. In the bright sunlight every age mark showed in her hands curled around the glass of tea.

"Good morning, GM." I set my coffee and bowl of cereal on the glass top of the table and plopped down in the chair across from her.

"Hello Keira." A faint smile lifted her face and her eyes sparkled watching me. "I see you're dressed for the outdoors today. How was your night in a strange new room?" Like Lawrence earlier, her eyes bored into me.

"It's strange, all right. You never told me I'd be sharing my room." I took a bite of cereal and watched her as I chewed.

Her only response was lifting her chin and peering at me, the smile still playing on her lips, waiting for me to continue.

"Yes, Molly has made her presence known. She's a real clean freak...picks up after me, whether I want her to or not." My eyes narrowed. "It might have been nice to let me know the house is haunted. But maybe you thought I wouldn't visit if I knew. Still, you could have prepared me when I got here."

"Molly?" She straightened in her chair and there was a bright grin on her lips, as she sat back. "Actually her name was Mary Clayburn...although I think Molly is a slang derivative of Mary."

My mouth paused in my chewing and I could only stare at her for a few moments before swallowing hard. It felt like a lump of coal burning its way down my tight throat. She even knew the woman's name and hadn't said word one about it before setting me up in that room!

"Are you shitting me?" I slammed the bowl down onto the table, my appetite now gone.

"Don't be vulgar, Keira. It doesn't become you." She leaned forward. "Of course I knew about Mary or Molly as you call her. She's made her presence known ever since I bought this house, many years ago. She worked as a maid in this house."

"Well that explains the cleaning obsession, I guess." If she was going to be casual about this, then I wasn't going to freak out and look silly. The ghost hadn't hurt me, only startled me...okay, scared the shit out of me, if I was being honest.

Grandmother set the glass of tea on the table and continued."Don't be callous. The first owner of the house, Lloyd Marshall, died and the home was to be sold. Mary had loved him for years, raised his children when his wife was stricken with T.B. and hospitalized. She couldn't bear the heartache and leaving the place where she'd lived and loved. She poisoned herself. She died a lonely woman."

My eyebrows drew together and I looked down into the steaming coffee. It was hard to be angry or even flippant about Molly after hearing that sad tale. To have loved someone that much that she ended her life when he died? That kind of love was hard to fathom.

"How do you know all this? Did you find her diary or something?" Even I knew that this kind of detail wouldn't be available in any research sources.

"Something like that. Yes." She plucked a stray white hair that had fallen onto her sleeve off and looked down her nose at it before flicking it away. "Why don't you try communicating with her? The poor thing is trapped here by her own doing. It can't be very much fun."

I just about choked on the coffee that I'd taken a large sip of. Communicate with Molly? What did I look like some kind of medium? Yeah, Keira Swanson, Ghost Whisperer at large?

"Why don't you? I mean, it's your house!" It was ridiculous to be even talking about this! Almost as crazy as a ghost maid hanging around my room.

"I've tried, believe me. Not for my sake but for hers. There're better places for her to be than mooning around this house." She straightened her collar and there was a smug, self satisfied look on her face when she looked over at me.

I was about to get up to take my bowl back to the kitchen and get a refill of coffee when a wave of dizziness made me hunch forward and clasp the edge of the table. When I looked over at GM there were two images of her sitting side by side. I blinked hard a few times to clear my eyes.

"Are you all right? You don't look well, Keira. You're pale." GM leaned forward and covered my hand with hers. Her touch was cool and dry on my skin.

"Just a dizzy spell." When I glanced at her, thankfully, there was only one GM this time. "Maybe my blood pressure is low or something." But the spell happening just after I'd finished a coffee that Lawrence had made wasn't lost on me. "I need a glass of water and some fresh air, I think."

GM tapped her cane on the stone floor a few times and Lawrence appeared in the doorway. "Would you mind clearing the dishes and getting Keira a glass of ice water, dear?"

His gaze shot to me and for just a moment there was a

hardness in his eyes, before a smile plastered his face. "Certainly." He moved forward and picked up the bowl and coffee mug.

"If it's not too much trouble, can I have a bottle of water?"

He paused. "The well water is fine, let me assure you. It's charcoal filtered and it's icy cold coming out of the fridge." He looked like I'd asked him for something exotic instead of just a bottle of water.

"That's fine. I'll get up and get it." I pushed past him and walked into the house. Tap water was fine but only if I poured it. I didn't trust Lawrence. And there'd been no mistake from the look he shot me that he resented the hell out of me being there.

As I stood at the fridge holding my glass under the spout for ice water, I noticed a thin notepad and pencil secured by a magnet. There were a few items already there and I picked up the pencil to add a case of bottled water to the list. It would be handier anyway, in case I went for a walk or tried out the boat. On second thought, I added 'Perrier' beside my entry.

I passed Lawrence as I walked out of the kitchen. The look in his eyes was still hard and he stepped back to let me pass. It was like I was so repugnant that he didn't even want to risk brushing up against me.

I couldn't resist getting in a shot at him. "Oh Lawrence...I've added bottled water to the list of groceries. Would you be a dear and put fresh limes on it too? I find gimlets so much better with fresh lime."

His eyebrows rose and he nodded curtly before pressing on into the kitchen. I couldn't help but smile.

GM turned from where she was plucking a dead leaf from a plant with a huge pink flower, and made as though she was rising to her feet before plopping back in the chair. "Would you mind taking some photos of the roses when we go outside?"

The air in the greenhouse room was still and sultry with the sun beaming its rays over the floor. I gulped the water down and then set the glass on the table. It would be good to get out into the fresh air, escaping the cloying warmth of the room. "Sure. Give me a minute and I'll be right back with my camera."

When I set foot on the flight of stairs to my floor, I wondered if Molly had tidied up my bed. The air on my bare legs and arms became colder the higher I climbed. It was so chilly that the hair on my arms tingled and goose bumps skittered down my spine.

Without warning, there was the sound of footsteps running across the floor of my bedroom, followed by a bump. A loud bump, almost a crashing noise.

I stopped short, my foot still on the step, half way up to my room. Whatever had raced across the floor and banged something shut wasn't Molly. Judging by the cold and the fact that my heart was galloping in my chest, this was a different entity altogether.

TEN

I stood still for another few beats, willing breath into my lungs and for my heart to slow down. If GM knew about Molly, she probably knew about this other ghost as well. It couldn't be dangerous. Right? I'd have to trust she wouldn't do that to me.

I leaned against the steep stairs and peeked over the top step to scan the room for ghosts, goblins, or whatever the hell else it could be. Why had my room become Ghost Central Station anyway? The house was plenty big to accommodate them in other rooms!

The sigh of frustration I let out formed a cloud vapor of front of me. Damn it was cold up here. I stood up on the stairs and ascended the rest of the way. At the top landing the temperature had dropped even more and I rubbed my arms.

Looking over my room, everything seemed normal. Well, as normal as it could be in this place. While my laptop was right where I left it, the clothes I had dropped on the floor earlier were now folded and on top of my dresser. My bed was made and even turned down again. But...

In the center of my bed was my camera—my expensive Canon T5 was lying on its side with the lens cap off.

"That's it!" I said out loud. I marched down to my bed. This was my room and my stuff! I didn't like anyone, dead or alive going through my things! I stopped in the center of the room. "Can't you people respect a person's privacy?" I said aloud.

I reached over to the bed to see that not only was the cap off, but the glowing red light showed that it had been left on. Next to it was an indentation on the bedding, evidence that someone or some thing had been sitting there playing with it.

This was definitely another ghost, not Molly. Not only did the room feel different somehow, no way would she leave the bed mussed.

I grabbed the camera and clicked the button on the back to display the pictures I'd already taken—the ones back home of the lake and swans in Central Park. As I scrolled through the images from home I squinted at the small screen. There were new pics.

And I didn't take them.

The first few were random, off kilter shots of the coffee table and floor. But the next one showed the face of a young boy. Under the large forehead, his eyes were ferret like dark slits, while his lips were drawn back in a snarl. Another showed only half his face, his lips loose and eyes open wide. His hair was cut very short and uneven, while the shirt he wore was a striped jersey. It reminded me of the kid in 'Home Alone'.

The hair on the back of my neck stood high all of a sudden. I wasn't alone in the room anymore. I turned my head slowly and then gasped. He was standing at the foot of my bed, glaring at me with eyes narrowed in anger. My heart leapt to my throat and an icy shiver crept down my spine.

We were both frozen in place staring at each other for what seemed like minutes but was probably only a few seconds. His image began to waver at the edges like the heat waves above a highway on a hot summer's day.

I took a deep breath, willing my voice from my throat

which was suddenly dry as dust. "Who are you?"

For a moment he was silent, and then he spoke.

"Sam." It was the high pitched voice of a young boy. He stepped back and the top of his pants, worn raggedy jeans came into view. He had to be only nine or ten years old from his size, but still, his sudden appearance made my blood run cold.

"What are you doing here?" I felt like I was in a dream—that this couldn't be happening. A ghost, a young boy was standing only a few feet away and I was asking him questions? And he was answering?

I crossed into the Twilight Zone from the first moment I entered this house.

"It's my room. Why are you here? Did Mama send you up?" His image faded a little and once more he took a step, or rather floated backward in retreat. His eyes now showed fear and his hands were fisted at his sides.

His Mama? What the heck was he talking about?

A flash of the room, a small iron bed and some wooden toys on the floor while the young boy stood looking out the window, appeared in my head and I jerked back. The vision and emotions that accompanied it was enough to tell me the story. Yes, this had been his room at one time. I sighed sadly. He died up here. I hadn't a clue how I knew this, but I'd stake my life on that fact.

The boy was watching me warily, with dark waves of fear emanating from his body. He was a prisoner here. He looked around at the room and when he turned to look at me again, the fear was now terror showing in the whites of his eyes.

"What happened to my room?" his voice was now shrill. "Where is my room?" The poor boy was now more scared than I was.

"This is my room now, Sam. You shouldn't be here." My voice had softened, barely above a whisper.

He looked frantic now, his gaze skimming over the room. His body shimmered becoming translucent so that I could see the wall behind him. And then he was gone.

I took a few ragged breaths and I gripped the camera tight. If not for the photos, I could pretend that this had been a dream, some kind of wacky hallucination. The temperature became warmer on my skin and I peered out the window at the bright day, a wisp of a cloud showing next to the sun. But it had happened. And what's more, GM knew about the spirits who haunted this room. What kind of sick sadist was she anyway?

The full weight of the implications of the episodes I experienced fell on me when I got to the top of the stairs and I grabbed the newel post for support as I gasped for breath.

There really are such things as ghosts!

I panted, trying to catch my breath. My entire picture of the world had just been ripped apart. Mom and Dad never went to church, they described themselves as committed agnostics. I enjoyed scary movies as much as the next girl, but now what had been the territory of Hollywood and Netflix… was folding my clothes and playing with my stuff?

If ghosts were real, then was God real? And if God was real, just how much trouble was I in for not going to church? And which God was it? Was he? Her? Should I be going to a mosque? A temple? An Ashram?

Oh man, this was a lot to take in for an afternoon. I looked down the staircase. Two floors down GM was sitting smug as the cat after the canary, and she'd been living in this place for years!

"One thing at a time, Kiera!" I said out loud. Great. I'm here two days and I'm talking to myself like an addled old woman. Just. Great.

Okay, then; one thing at a time. Fine. First Molly and now Sam. Both had lived in the house, specifically in my room. They were tied to that room somehow. G.M had said why not talk to Molly? Well, I'd tried that with Sam and I wasn't sure if it helped either of us. For sure, I was moving from that room…if not out of the house entirely! Sam and Molly were welcome to it.

As I emerged from the stairwell to the second floor, I

glanced down the hall where the other guest bedrooms were. I could move in there, but there was no guarantee that the same thing wouldn't happen again. The place was old and probably lots of people over the years had died in it. Who knew what kind of entity would show up?

When I entered the sunroom, GM was still sitting in her wicker chair. She looked up and her eyes examined me like an ant under a magnifying glass. I shook my head from side to side and plopped down in the chair across from her. This was unreal. I just saw a ghost—my second ghost, and now I was going to chat about it with my grandma! I looked at her, my eyes narrowing. She knew something had happened...probably that's why she wanted pictures of her roses. Any excuse for me to go back upstairs. This bitch set me up!

"Keira? What's happened?" She leaned forward and her fingers covered mine.

I yanked my hand away from her and spat the words out. "You know what happened! That's why you wanted me to go upstairs to get the camera. You knew there'd be another ghost to scare the hell out of me!"

Her mouth was a straight, inscrutable line as she watched me. "Yes?"

"That's it? That's the only thing you've got to say about this!" Her passive posture, the acceptance of all this like I was discussing the weather or some inane thing was maddening. I grabbed the camera and pulled up the photo of the boy on the small screen. I thrust it at her. "Here! Is that who you thought I'd meet? How many other ghosts do you have up your sleeve?"

I looked wildly around the room waiting for Casper to pop out of a wall. No, nothing. Okay, so far so good. I turned back to GM.

She glanced at the camera and then her fingers tugged at the cuff of her shirt. She leaned over to peer inside. "Nothing up my sleeve." When she chuckled, I was tempted to jump out of my seat and throttle her.

"Laugh if you want, but I'm out of here! I don't care if I

have to hitch-hike home but I'm not staying!" I held my tongue from telling her what a sadistic bitch I thought she was. She owed me an explanation if nothing else before I left.

The worst of it was, I'd have to go back into that room to pack my stuff. I shoved my feet out and crossed my arms over my chest, slumping down into the seat.

"If you're through having your tantrum, I'll explain it to you." She rose to her feet, steadying herself with her hands pressing the top of the cane. "Well? Come along and take some shots of my roses. I'll tell you all about it, outside in the sunshine." The corners of her mouth twitched upwards and her chin rose.

"My hand shot up and I pointed at the ceiling. "There's ghosts in my bedroom! And you want to take pictures of flowers? Are you insane?" Why bother to ask? The woman was totally bonkers.

GM's head tilted at me, an annoyed expression on her face. "Not bonkers, young lady. Experienced. Now, let's go."

I huffed out a breath and followed.

What the hell else could I do?

ELEVEN

When I stepped outside, looking over the expanse of green lawn, anywhere but at my grandmother, the sun was warm on my face. In the distance, the rays sparkled on the small waves of the river, while a sailboat floated by.

Her hand skimmed over my arm and landed in the crook of my elbow, tugging me closer. "First of all, this is your home, so there's no hitch-hiking away from it."

"No, it's not. It's your home and you've got two, too many residents for my liking." That was generous on my part. I'd only met two of the ghosts when there was probably an army of them. I slowed my gait to accommodate her. She was after all, pretty old, even if I could have throttled her.

"I'm leaving the house as well as the bulk of my fortune to you, Keira." She stopped, her eyes large and solemn, watching me.

My mouth fell open. GM barely knew me and she wanted me to inherit? Not that I wanted any part of this house, but the fortune...well, that could solve some problems. "What? I don't understand. Why me and not Mom?"

"I said 'the bulk'. Your parents will be well provided for, don't worry." She turned and motioned with her chin for us to continue to her precious rose garden. "I told you before, you are special, Keira. Your mother, much as I love her, didn't inherit your abilities." She glanced over at me and smiled. "Take Sam. It was a very long time before he showed himself to me. But with you it was only a couple of days. That shows real promise."

"Thanks." This time it was me who ground to a halt. What the hell was I doing, thanking her for scaring the hell out of me? "Wait a minute. You knew I'd encounter Molly, but Sam was some kind of test? Is that it?" This was insane. Who did this kind of thing? And to their granddaughter of all people!

"Yes. As crazy as it might seem, you passed the test. As for the house, we'll talk about your inheritance in more detail soon. First, I need to know what transpired between Sam and you."

I chewed this over in my mind for a few moments. I had just been hit with a one two punch and had to process it. I stand to inherit millions, I'm sure; and on top of that, my meeting Sam was some kind of test? Test for what? My head was spinning.

"Keira." GM touched me. "Just tell me what happened between the two of you."

I blinked a couple of times. "I asked him his name and he told me. He wanted to know if his mother had sent me. I told him that the room was now mine and he should leave." My eyebrows bunched together when I remembered the vision that flashed in my mind. "I saw the room for a moment the way it had been, when he lived there. He was kind of like a prisoner there." I sighed. How was that possible for a young boy like him? Yet the fear in his eyes had been real.

GM squeezed my arm and leaned closer. The scent of roses drifted into my nose from her proximity. "He was a prisoner. A hundred years ago, when a child wasn't right in the head, they were often locked away. Sam had bouts of schizophrenia and was kept up there, away from the other children."

I knew the answer to my next question, but needed to hear it from her own lips. The day had gone completely still around us; the sounds of birds chirping and the breeze in the trees faded as we talked. This was too weird for words. I looked at her from under my eyelashes. "And you know this...how?"

She smiled sweetly. "I talked to him, of course. That's also how I found out Mary...I mean Molly's story." She paused for a moment, giving me an appraising look. "You did the right thing, asking him to leave. Your instincts were right on."

"So he's gone? For good?" I blew out a huff of air. "Well, that's a relief."

"I'd be surprised if that was all it took." Her blossomed into a grin and her eyes twinkled at me. "Keira, what do you know about the afterlife?"

I looked past her at the house. "A hell of a lot more than I did a couple of days ago, that's for sure." I returned my gaze to her. "What do you mean, GM?"

"Did you believe ghosts existed before coming here?"

I chewed my lip. "No, not really." I looked away and added, "But I wanted to. I mean, I kind of wished they did."

"Why?"

I had to think that one over for a few seconds. "Because... if they exist... then we never really die." I nodded my head. "Ghosts prove that there's life after death, don't they?"

GM nodded, "You drew a good conclusion from the evidence at hand, Keira. Well done."

I didn't admit to her then, and wish I could have, that her approval made me feel good. "But then... why don't we see them all the time, GM?"

"Bingo." She pointed her fingers at me like she was shooting a gun. "That's the next good question. Why is that, do you think?"

"I don't know... but I'll bet you a million bucks you got some ideas."

She nodded. "You're right, I do. I don't have all the answers, but I do have some." She cocked her head back to the big house. "Molly... and Sam... you saw their 'spirits'... their 'souls' if you want to use that term. Whatever word you use, you're describing that part of us..." she paused and held my arm. "The part of us that moves on." She glanced back at the house and then back at me. "I believe it's the energy in us that is truly just us" She tapped my chest. "There is an energy in you that is only Keira, dear." Tapping her own chest, she added, "Just as there is an energy in me that is just me. It's this energy that moves on to another plane of existence after one's body dies."

"So when I saw those ghosts, I was actually seeing their souls?"

"I prefer the term spirit, but yes—the fundamental essence of their nature that transcends their bodies."

"Yeah. That makes sense to me. I mean, I remember from school that they say energy can never be destroyed. It might transform but it still is." My brain was just beginning to ache now. I'm no intellectual; the deepest discussions I'm used to are who's hotter Johnny Depp or Brad Pitt. (Just so you know, it's Ryan Gosling).

GM was watching me as the wheels turned in my head. Then it hit me. "It's like in the movies and books!" I said. "The ghosts I see are ones that are stuck here!"

She clapped her hands, smiling. "Now you're getting to the heart of the matter!" She put her hand around my waist and we continued down the path of the garden. "There is a thin curtain separating life as we know it and the next plane of existence, Keira. The spirits of some people get caught in that fabric, like a fly behind a window sheer. They're stuck between here and eternity. They're supposed to move on, but sometimes people are too rooted in the life they've led." She gave a small shrug. "Sometimes they don't know they've even left the living."

I came to a stop. "How do you know this GM? I mean, you sound so certain about all this."

"It's been my life's work, Keira. I see spirits." She held up a finger. "I mean, occasionally other people are able to as well, but only when those spirits reveal themselves. But for me I'm much more attuned to them. I experience souls who are marooned."

"Marooned?"

"Yes. They're tied to this world when they should have moved on." She was silent for a few moments, watching me try to digest this.

"Oh, you're some kind of Ghostbuster?"

She rolled her eyes at me. "Oh, you're sooo original! I've never heard that one before!" She shot a peeved look back at the house. "When that stupid movie came out, Laurence played that theme song night and day for a month!"

I crossed my arms. "But you are, right?"

She waggled her eyebrows at me. "More like a 'Ghost Whisperer' actually. I nudge them along to the next plane where they belong. Sometimes it's really hard when they fear that level. It's still an unknown for them as well as us. And it gets a lot more…" she cleared her throat, "complicated if they've lived a bad life, because they're afraid that they're going to hell."

"Is there? Is there a heaven and a hell?" I still had my arms crossed, because I hadn't asked the big question yet.

Her face took on a thoughtful look as she shook her head slowly. "To tell the truth, I really don't know for sure. I've not yet gone to the other side of The Veil. I believe it's a better place, and I'm convinced it's where we belong after we die."

"So you've made it your life's work to help people cross over this veil thingy."

"Yes. Now ask your question out loud." She gazed at me with steady eyes.

"Why? Why can't they stay here if they want to? Who are you to get them to move on?"

"And that's the $64,000.00 question, isn't it?"

"Why sixty four thousand?"

She gave a small wave. "Just an old fashioned figure of speech dear. Before your time." She slowly blinked and went on. "It's a question of balance."

"Balance? What does that mean?"

"It's how the universe works. A caterpillar can't stay a caterpillar. It has to become a butterfly." She pointed at me. "You couldn't remain a child for all time, you had to follow the path of Nature, which is the path of the Universe. Just as you had to learn to walk and talk..." she arched an eyebrow, "and go through puberty; these spirits need to move on. It's what the Universe needs to maintain balance."

"How do you know that? What makes you so sure? Maybe these ghosts do belong here?"

She shook her head vigorously. "Absolutely not; I learned that the hard way."

"Oh? What happened?"

"That story is for another time, perhaps. For now, you just need to understand this: we're meant to go from this plane to the next one. The Veil that separates the living and the dead is delicate. Too many spirits on this side weakens it." GM took a deep breath. "It's not just pushing souls along for their own well being Keira, it affects us all, the living as well as the dead. The universe depends on this separation. Time and space become affected."

She was losing me. I could understand wanting a better realm for spirits caught in the middle but time and space? "So what happens? I mean, if too many linger? Aside from haunting the rest of us, scaring the living daylights out of us, how bad can it get?" I looked down at the grass. Also, why were Molly and Sam still in her house if she was so good at this?

"It can get a whole lot worse than it is right now, let me tell you." Her jaw tightened and she pointed to a red rose that was still tight in the bud, only the outer petals curling to the sun. "That one is in my favourite stage. Get a shot of that, will you?"

When I stepped away from her and lifted the camera, rotating the lens to zoom in, she continued. "Just like in your camera when Sam's spirit played with it. He took a picture—"

"Yeah, spooky selfie," I snickered.

"Keira! This is serious!" I was taken aback by her vehemence. "An image of a spirit is captured in your camera. It's evidence that The Veil is thin that it could be photographed like that. Can you imagine the chaos if there were many, many more of these spirits roaming around? It would affect the nature of reality!"

I lowered my camera. "What the hell is that supposed to mean? 'The nature of reality'. Really, GM, you sound like some Buddha dude or something."

She sighed. "This is a little tricky to explain. What time is it?"

I glanced at my watch. "It's 11:45."

"And right now it's a few seconds after that, right?" When I nodded, she said, "There is no time on the other side of The Veil, Keira. It's an Eternal state. There is only a 'now'. On the other side, there's no tomorrow, nor yesterday... just a now."

"So it's 11:45 all the time over there?"

"And 10:15, and Midnight, and 5:00 pm—and all at the same instant."

"That's crazy. How can that be?"

"For the sake of argument, just try to accept that on the other side of The Veil, nobody has to worry about being late. Time as we understand it does not exist on that side." She tilted her head. "Now the next part is really going to blow your mind. There's no space as we know it on that side either."

"Space? Like in Star Wars?"

She shook her head 'No'. "No, I mean there is no 'here' nor 'there'. In the Eternal, those basic ways we deal with existence do not apply."

My head started to hurt right behind my left eye; it was like I was back in High School trying to understand Algebra.

GM saw the expression on my face and kept going anyway. "Listen to me. What do you think would happen to this world," she spread her arms, "if there was no 'Now' or 'Then' or 'Here' or 'There'?"

My eyes flew open wide as an image of the world—cites and forests, mountains and oceans folding and blending into each other, creating some kind of vortex of destruction—flashed in my mind. I gasped. Every living thing, dying in the most terrifying way imaginable. No, not dying... "Ceasing to exist," I whispered. I staggered; my camera dropping to the ground as I held my head, trying to catch my breath.

"Yes, Keira...ceasing to exist."

"Wait a minute!" My hand shot out and I pointed at her. "You put that vision in my head!"

GM shook her head slowly. "No Keira, my abilities lie in being able to share what you're thinking, yes; but I'm unable to put thoughts into your mind. I felt you experiencing it, yes; I saw it in your head, but that vision you had was like the one you had in your bedroom of Sam's past life. I didn't put those there."

"But... but how did I see it then?" I was still trying to catch my breath from the horror of it all. I've seen planets destroyed tons of times in the movies... but I felt this utter destruction!

GM stepped up to me and put her arms around me. "It's because you are very much like me, dear. Very, very much like me." She held me to her and began to rub my back. "The vision has passed now, Keira... you're safe." She guided me to a lawn bench that was nearby and sat us both down on it. Still stroking my back, she gave a small laugh. "When I had that vision the first time, I fainted." Hugging me she said, "You got angry! You're a very strong woman, do you know that?"

Strong? I felt as weak as a kitten.

"Yes, strong. And we're not finished." She tilted my face towards her own. "My mission has been to protect The Veil. To keep that premonition you just had from happening. If too many spirits stay on this side of it, their 'Eternal-ness' will disrupt this side." She took a breath and spoke softly, "And probably the other side as well."

"Reality."

"Yes. Reality."

My head hung to my side, resting on her own. "So you want me to help you save the Universe."

"More or less."

"Oh."

We sat silently holding hands.

***

I had closed my eyes for a few minutes. I didn't think about what GM just told me, it was too big. I just let my thoughts float around aimlessly.

I sat up with a jerk and turned to her. "Ghostbusting doesn't pay well, does it?"

She snorted. "I hate that term! No, it really doesn't."

My eyes narrowed. "But you're a whiz at investing?"

"I've had some help."

"Oh?"

"I know where you're going, Keira. Yes, I've had help from someone from the other side."

"The stock market. You somehow use spirits to get stock tips?"

She laughed and it was like a bell tinkling. "Gives a whole new meaning to insider trading, doesn't it?" At my shocked expression, her chin lowered and she smiled. "I only did it to have the freedom for pursuing my real work. But, I guess we can justify anything if we put our mind to it." She laughed again.

"Time doesn't really exist on that plane. In life, we think in linear terms...the past, present and the future. But there, it doesn't exist. My friend, Ralph, had worked the markets all his life. His interest didn't die with his body. He enjoyed giving me information, tips, which made me very wealthy." She pointed to the house. "He was here for years and years before he moved on. Sort of like Sam and Molly, except he stayed here for my sake, not because he didn't want to move on. After he moved on, I hired living investment managers. The rest is history."

I straightened, looking over at her again. "That was interfering in time...and even space, what you did. Is this what you meant? But the world didn't collapse or anything when you did it. So what was the harm?"

"You have a point. But I'm a single, isolated case, and Ralph did move on when I was financially set."

"Puts a whole new spin on 'Angel Investor'," I smirked.

GM got a far away look in her eyes. "Hmm... I never thought of that... maybe he was..." She cleared her throat and her face became solemn. "Keira. Imagine if there were hundreds like me short circuiting the financial markets? It would be chaotic. My ultimate goal was altruistic. Could the same be said of most people?"

"No. All you have to do is read how corporations are causing havoc as it is, GM."

"I shudder at the thought of some Wall Street hedge fund manager with that sort of information," she said. "The economy and state of the world is bad enough as it is, don't you think?"

I recalled that derelict at the subway station last week. Wealthiest city on the planet and he didn't have socks. "Yeah," I sighed. "But...speaking of wealth... the inheritance...I still don't know what it is you want of me. I mean...there's got to be a catch." Call me cynical but she'd offered that inheritance pretty damned fast when I said I was going to leave.

For a long moment she watched me silently, her gaze soft meeting mine. "I don't offer this lightly, Keira. If there was any other way, believe me I'd jump at the chance to take it. Don't get me wrong. My work with safeguarding The Veil has been infinitely rewarding. I have helped many people, both living and dead. But, I'm not without enemies doing this. Powerful enemies. Here and in the next plane of existence."

A shiver went down my spine despite the warmth of the day. If I was to carry on her life's work which she had intimated was her intention, then I'd not only inherit her wealth, I'd inherit her enemies too.

TWELVE

Later, we sat in the sunroom eating a lunch of toasted tomato sandwiches and tossed garden salad. All thoughts of exploring the grounds and river were abandoned with her revelations in the rose garden.

Lawrence had only appeared long enough to serve lunch before muttering something about catching up with the laundry. Did he know about the inheritance? That she'd made me her heir? I still wasn't sure about him but for the time being, there were more important things to think about than her elderly 'Guy Friday'.

"So tell me more about these enemies of yours. I mean, they must be pretty scary if you sent Mom away for her protection." I looked down into the bowl of leafy green lettuce and cucumber, toying with it as I spoke. I still wasn't sure I was going to agree to any of this...not until I knew what I was up against.

GM dabbed the corners of her mouth and set the napkin back on her lap. "I can't tell you their names. In all honesty, I don't know that. If I did, well, it would be so much simpler.

But, I know when they are close." Her face had dropped and there was an iron glint in her eyes.

"But why? Why would anyone, here or in the next stage of existence want to stop you? Is it the money? Some greedy people who want to do what you did...use the next plane for profit on the stock market? Or even power?" My lips twitched as I pictured a Darth Vader type or even Dr. Evil in the Austin Powers movie.

Her chin rose and she smiled. "If it were only so. That, I could easily deal with. No. I'm afraid that it's anarchy that they desire. The end of everything as we know it. They've come close a few times and I barely escaped with my sanity, let alone my life. "

The doorbell rang.

I jerked in my chair and stared at her. Her eyes mirrored mine. We were both thinking the same thing. *Was it them?*

Her hand went to her throat and she sighed. "Can you get that, Keira? Lawrence is upstairs and he might not have heard it."

"Are you expecting anyone?" I forced my heart back down from where it had leapt into my throat. All this talk about enemies and the supernatural was getting to me.

She shook her head 'no'.

"Okaay. Be right back." As I was leaving the room the bell rang again. "Hold on!" I pulled the door open and there stood a woman, around my own age in a white uniform shirt and navy shorts. In her hand was an envelope and an electronic clipboard. Her head pulled back and her grey eyes were almost as round as mine, staring back at me.

"Hi. I've got a registered letter for Mrs. York. Is she around?" Her brown hair was tied up in a pony tail but a few stray wisps framed the sides of her face. A smattering of freckles crossed the ridge of a small nose above a tentative grin.

I reached out to take the letter from her. "That's my grandmother. I can sign for her." It was weird. I was already feeling like the lady of the Manor.

She handed it to me and then lifted the gadget, clicking the plastic pen on the smooth surface. "Sign here." Her eyes were filled with question marks looking at me. "I'm Gwen Jones. I've been delivering mail here for years and I've never seen you before. Is Lawrence okay?"

I chuckled seeing her confusion as I scratched my signature on her board. "He's fine. He's just busy right now. I'm Keira Swanson. This is my first visit from New York."

Her eyebrows rose and she nodded. "Oh! Well, that's nice." She dodged to the side and peeked into the foyer. "I haven't seen your grandmother or Lawrence in a while. The odd time I see her outside, clipping leaves from her plants. She's nice. I like your grandmother."

I laughed at her sneaking a peek around me. What did she think? That this was some 'home invasion' and they were tied up in some room behind me? "Yeah. She's pretty cool." I wasn't going to add anything about Lawrence. "Thanks." I started to close the door, where she was still trying to examine behind me.

"Yeah. Yeah, right. Have a good day!" I closed the door and as I walked back through the foyer, Lawrence's voice called out.

"Who was that, Keira?" He stood at the railing on the second floor, staring down at me.

I waved the letter high in my hand. "Just the mail lady. She gave me a registered letter for GM" I continued on my way but could hear him muttering as he stepped back.

"GM indeed," he sniffed.

Whatever. When I entered the sun room GM was gazing down at her plate, totally in her own world. "It was just the mail lady...Gwen. She asked about you." I tossed the letter next to her plate.

Ignoring it, she smiled. "She's a nice girl." She folded her hands on her lap and cleared her throat. "Keira? In my bedroom is a small embroidered pillow on my loveseat. Would you mind getting it for me?"

I blinked and then popped to my feet once more. "Sure

thing."

I made my way over to her bedroom and went in. A large bed with a red satin spread sat against the far wall, while a set of French doors next to it showed the side of the property and her rose garden. When I stepped inside, the wall opposite her bed showed a floor to ceiling wall of shelves filled with books. The loveseat sofa sat next to it and sure enough, there was a blue pillow embroidered with white flowers, tucked into the arm. Unlike the other rooms, my feet sank into wall to wall beige carpeting as I strode over to get the pillow. The air in the room was warm with an overlay of the scent of roses.

When I picked up the pillow, I stopped short. A wave of dizziness washed through my head and I grasped the arm of the sofa. The image of an old woman, her white hair swept back from a tanned and wrinkled face flashed in my mind. Her eyes were small and dark like a bird's behind thick glasses that perched on her fleshy nose. Sadness flooded through me and I hugged the pillow into my leaden stomach.

The pillow was the last Mother's Day gift from her son. He'd given it to her and then boarded the train with the other troops. It was the last time she saw him. A tear rolled down my cheek and I brushed it away with the back of my hand. The old woman had held that pillow and spilled many tears into the old tattered fabric.

I took a deep breath and counted to ten. What was happening to me? The woman had felt so real in my head, her sorrow consuming me. This had never happened with any other object I'd touched. My shoulders squared and I walked back out of the room. GM had known about the pillow. It was another one of her 'tests'. But instead of fear, this time the emotion was sorrow.

As I walked under the set of stairs, still clutching the pillow the name Helen and then Jeremy popped into my head. The mother and her son. My forehead was furrowed trying to puzzle this out. Why now? Why had this never happened before if I had this so called gift?

When I stepped into the sun room, GM's head rose and her

eyes focused on mine. She also looked sad...but more than that, she looked tired and old. The bit of colour that had been in her cheeks when we were outside earlier and at lunch had faded and there was a grey pallor to her skin.

I paused, staring into her eyes. "Helen and Jeremy. But you knew that, didn't you?"

She nodded and then leaned forward. "Can you put the pillow behind me?"

When I tucked the pillow in, more of her hair had escaped the French roll like she'd just got out of bed or something. "You knew I'd feel Helen's sadness didn't you?" It was still there actually, sitting like a lump, low in my gut.

"I'd hoped." She sat back, a small smile turning her lips. "You not only have clairvoyance but you have psychometric ability. Just touching the pillow, you were able to know the story behind it."

I took a seat and hunched forward looking at her. "But why now, GM? I've never done this before." In all the time in New York, never once had I seen a spirit or touched objects and got mental movies from them. This was beyond weird. I felt wobbly, like I'd drunk a bottle of wine but my mind was still clear.

"I bought this place because of the psychic energy in this house...on the grounds. If any of your gifts were to emerge, I knew it would happen here." Her hand closed over mine and she squeezed it. "Even the pillow...I picked it up in an antique store, but with you in mind." Her eyes closed for a minute and it looked like she was dozing off.

"GM? Are you all right?" My eyes opened wider as a surge of concern filled me. She was old...and she looked worn out right then.

Her eyes fluttered open and she grasped her cane, banging it on the floor a few times. "Keira. I'm afraid that I'll need to lay down now. All of this has tired me." She smiled. "I'm pleased with you. We'll talk again at dinner."

Lawrence appeared and his face was flushed from the speed that he'd taken to get there so quick. His eyes narrowed, peering at me like I'd done something horrid to GM. He rushed forward and his hand cupped her shoulder. "Are you okay, Pamela?"

She looked up at him and smiled. "Of course, dear. Just tired is all. I'll go for my nap early today." She rose to her feet and I watched the two of them, hunched and plodding like exhausted pack animals leave the room.

The blue upholstered pillow sat in the chair like an accusation.

My shoulders drooped lower. That poor woman, Helen, had cherished the pillow, the last gift from her son. Since I'd been there I'd only sent one text to my mother—something that was as easy as breathing in this day and age. Just as Jeremy had been Helen's only child, I was Mom's only child.

With a sigh of guilt, I pulled my cell phone from my pocket. Of course, now that I wasn't planning on leaving I had a full signal. My fingers flew over the keypad. It was just a quick note to let her know I hadn't dropped off the face of the earth and that well...despite sending me to GM's house, I still loved her. I glanced over at the cushion and rose to my feet. *There! I sent a text to my Mother, okay?'*

Having dealt with the Helen and Jeremy guilt pillow, I stretched and sighed again. This house and everything GM had told me today was closing in on me. Ghosts in my bedroom, guilt pillows, and saving reality all in one day. This place was starting to press in on me. I needed a dose of normal like a junkie needed a fix. Plus, I hadn't been out of the house in two days!

I raced upstairs, slowing down when I got to the few steps below my room. Taking a deep breath, I walked up and scanned the sitting area from one side to the other. There were no ghosts and things were exactly as I had left them. I changed out of the shorts and threw a pair of jeans on.

"You'll take care of my shorts, won't you, Molly?" So weird. Having a ghostly maid.

I picked up my purse and slung the strap over my shoulder. There was still twenty dollars in it—enough to buy me a coffee when I got to the city. Surely, there would be a Starbucks...and some people close to my age hanging around there. I'd leave a note for Lawrence that I borrowed the car. If I didn't, he'd probably be on the phone so fast it'd make your head spin and there'd be an all points police warrant or something out on me.

Just a short sanity break, a chance to catch my breath.

Lord knows, I'd earned it.

THIRTEEN

With the window rolled down and the radio blasting, I manoeuvred the land yacht down the highway, breaking the speed limit if not the sound barrier. The wind lifted my hair and my fingers kept a steady beat on the leather clad steering wheel. Freedom!

I entered the city limits, cruising past an army base. On the left was a sign—*Royal Military College*. Hmm...Their version of West Point? Hot guys in uniforms? Things were looking up already.

I crossed a bridge and was in the heart of downtown Kingston. Compared to New York it was pretty small; you could fit the downtown core with its few high rises into Central Park and not even notice it was there. Still, it was a city; I could feel myself relaxing into the bustle. I'm a city girl through and through. A country setting's nice and all, but I feel more at home with sidewalks and traffic lights.

When I cruised down the main street I spotted the universal green sign with the mermaid wearing a crown and smiled. It even says 'Starbucks' in Canada! Yes! I could almost taste the cinnamon in the latte as I searched the street for a parking spot.

I found a space on the block just past the coffee shop and parked the car. Just as I pulled the door open, someone called my name and I spun around.

"Keira?"

Coming up the walkway was a brunette in a white shirt and navy shorts waving 'hi'. The mail lady? What was her name? Gwen, that was it.

"Hi Gwen." The last thing I expected when I walked down the street in this city was to meet someone I *knew*. Talk about a small city...

I was still holding the door open and she grinned at me. "This is my after work ritual. Nothing says you're finished for the day better than a butterscotch latte."

"No way! Cinnamon's the best, even if I didn't spend the day working." I held the door open for her and followed inside.

The smell of fresh roasted coffee filled the air as I looked around, checking the place out. It was doing a steady business with the under thirty set. Gwen turned and her voice was low. "There're still lots of students in the city even though it's summer break." Her dark eyes flitted across the room. "I see an empty table. Want to join me?"

I smiled. "Sure." We were close in age and it would be a welcome change from the octogenarian set. I watched her turn to give our orders to the guy behind the counter. She spun quickly and grinned. "It was cinnamon latte right?"

When I nodded she continued. "Coffee's on me. Consider it a welcome to the city gesture."

"Thanks." In just a minute the server set the two cups of frothy drinks on the counter. We made our way to the empty table near the large window over-looking the street.

She tugged the chair out and set her latte on the small wooden table. "So how long are you in town, Keira?"

I took a seat and emptied a bit of sugar into the hot cup. "I don't know." I looked down into my coffee, stirring it. It was a good question. Could be, I'd never leave or I might be gone tomorrow. But I couldn't tell her that. "I came here to look after my grandmother, but to be honest, she seems pretty healthy. I mean, Mom made it sound like she was on death's door."

Gwen took a sip of her drink and her eyebrows rose high. "You too, huh? I take care of my dad. He's had M.S. for years but now it's progressed to the point that he can't work anymore."

The smile dropped from my lips. "I'm sorry to hear that. That must be rough." I couldn't imagine if my parents weren't healthy. Dealing with GM was one thing; she was old, but Gwen's dad was probably a lot younger.

She looked down, slowly stirring the foam into the dark mixture. "He's not completely helpless but it's hard for him walking. My brother spells me off sometimes, so that helps." She brightened and managed a smile. "So what's it like living in your grandmother's house? I've always wondered what it'd be like inside. The grounds are gorgeous, I can only imagine how...how *elegant,* it would be on the inside."

I nodded. "It's straight out of Downton Abbey—high plaster ceilings, wooden paneling all over the place, hardwood floors..." I leaned in. "And the bathrooms have those huge claw foot tubs you can almost swim in!"

"Yep. I was right; it sounds elegant."

I nodded. "Yeah, and it has a beautiful view of the river from her sunroom. That's her favourite room in the house. You can see the river flowing to Lake Ontario from it. We have breakfast and lunch there."

She chuckled. "That doesn't surprise me. Judging by the gardens, she's got a real green thumb. I'm sure Lawrence does a lot to help...how else could she manage that huge house?" Her eyes met mine over the rim.

"Yeah. He's pretty devoted to her." I grimaced and looked down into my own latte. "Me, not so much."

"What do you mean? You don't get along with your

grandmother? She's—"

"No, not her; she's fine. A little eccentric, but at her age she's earned it, I guess. Let's just say that Lawrence isn't my biggest fan." I wasn't going to get into my suspicions over him wanting GM's inheritance.

Her mouth pulled to the side in a small smirk. "Well, old people get set in their ways, I guess; he's been with her for years and years and you just showed up." She looked out the window and waved to a middle aged man, also in the postal garb. He was getting into his car and waved back.

When she turned back and smiled, I spoke, "So, do you like delivering mail?"

"It's okay. It wasn't the career I studied for but it's probably worked out better than being a physicist."

"A physicist?"

"Yeah," she smiled as she started toying with her napkin. "Theoretical Physics to be precise."

"I didn't even take physics in high school. All that math and stuff…"

Gwen waved her hand, dismissively. "Yeah, I got game when it comes to math; but I really sucked at writing papers." She looked away. "It was pretty cool though. We were doing some backup work here at Queen's University for the Higg's boson project in Europe when I left."

"The what?"

She was still staring out the window. "They called it the search for 'The God Particle'." She turned back to me, her eyes bright. "And they found it!" She shook her head. "When I left, I was just about to wrap up my Master's and I was going back and forth whether to work in that area or String Theory for my Doctorate." She shrugged. "But life made my decision for me."

"What happened?"

"My Dad got sick. Well… sicker. It got so bad he had to stop working. His disability pension isn't enough to live on, so I got the job with the Post Office. I had been part time when I was in school, so it was easier for me to grab a full time slot when it opened up." She shrugged again. "So here I am."

My academic efforts, as scattered as they were, seemed small time. The woman delivering our mail was a Brainiac. I felt for her. She had something she had worked on for years and had to give it up, and I couldn't even finish a course in photography. "I'm sorry to hear that," I said.

She shrugged again. "It's really not that big a deal. The pay and benefits are okay, and I'm done by three so I can be home to look after Dad." She pointed her chin at me. "How about you? What do you do when you're not visiting your grandmother?" There was an easy way about Gwen. She'd asked like she was really interested rather than being in some kind of pissing contest.

I made a crooked smile. "I'm an under-achiever. I tried my hand at social work, photography and my latest venture was in acting school. I pretty much got booted out of everything I tried." I could just about laugh now about my parents kicking me out of the nest. The nest I'd landed in—if I decided to stay, that is—was pretty feathered.

"You just haven't found your passion yet. That's all." Her face had turned serious and she leaned over the table folding her hands primly together.

I couldn't help the chuckle that bubbled in my throat at her words. "Seriously? C'mon Gwen. You can't tell me that delivering mail is your passion." Talk about under-achiever, especially if she'd studied physics.

She took a breath and her head fell to the side, looking down at the table. "No… but it's my job." She lifted her eyes at me. "My family's my passion."

My cheeks flared hotly and I looked down into the cup of coffee. "Sorry about that crack. You did the right thing. Life sucks sometimes, doesn't it?" I couldn't imagine looking after an aging parent and worrying about money. "So it's just you and your Dad living together?"

"Yup. My brother, Sean, lives in Toronto. He's a Customs Broker. I was always closer to my Dad anyway, so it made sense for me to look after him." She shrugged her shoulders and smiled. "It works for all of us."

She hadn't mentioned anything about her mother and I wasn't asking. I'd already put my foot in my mouth once. "So, what do you do for fun? I noticed that military college. Must be lots of guys around here." She also hadn't mentioned a boyfriend. Maybe we could hit the night life sometime, even if she was worlds away from Cerise and the Greenwich Village club scene. Gwen wore very little make-up and she certainly didn't need it, not with those eyes.

Her eyebrows bobbed high before she tucked a lock of hair behind her ear. "There's no shortage of single men in this town, that's for sure. In addition to the Military College there's a huge military base in Kingston." Her lips pulled back in a small grimace. "I'm not into the bar scene though."

I smiled thinking of Cerise and me hitting nightclubs until four in the morning. It seemed like another lifetime now. "So what do you do for fun?" I took a sip of the latte and smiled. Surely there was something fun to do in this town.

"I swim, read, and play with the dog." Her face flushed and she blurted it out. "There's the odd date...meeting someone on-line but that hasn't worked out too well, so far. Lots of frogs but no princes. How about you? "

Well that answered one question, although my gay-dar hadn't picked up any vibes. "Different swamp but same old frogs although some of them were more like alligators. I had a boyfriend for about a year but we broke up." A picture of Barry flashed in my mind. Was he still seriously hooked on Minecraft? It had gotten boring being with a man-child.

"You know, I don't live that far from your grandmother's. You should come over for a swim in the pool."

That could be fun. She seemed O.K., and having a friend close by would be a welcome break to my routine with GM. "My grandmother takes a nap every afternoon. I like to spend time with her, but anytime after four, I'm free."

"Hey! That's perfect then. My house is the white clapboard farm house, about a ten minute walk past yours but on the opposite side of the road. You'll see 'Jones' on the blue mailbox. Come by tomorrow for a drink and a swim." She glanced at the watch on her wrist and then sighed. "I'd better get going. I promised Dad I'd take him to the casino after work. It's our Friday night ritual—a prime rib dinner and the slots. He just about breaks even most times."

"He ever think about playing poker there?" If GM went with him, it would sure increase his odds of winning. If she could have one of her ghosts tag along and peek at the cards for her. I smiled mischievously at the thought. "Well, thanks for the coffee. Next time, the treat's on me."

She rose to her feet and flipped a few coins on the table for a tip. "So, I'll see you around four tomorrow?" She had a genuine smile when she looked down at me.

"Absolutely! Good luck at the casino."

She shook her head and laughed. "Wait till I tell him I met Mrs. York's granddaughter! He'll be thrilled. That house is a bit of a legend around here."

My eyebrows pulled together and my smile faltered. My grandmother's words rang in my ear, '*I bought this house for its psychic energy*'. Did everyone know about it? "What? What do you mean?"

"I'll tell you tomorrow! It was nice meeting you. Gotta run." She turned and wound her way through the tables and customers. Her hand rose in a wave and then she was out the door.

I held the paper coffee cup between my hands and looked down at the lacy remnants of foam still clinging to the inside. Now that I was alone, my mind wandered back to the morning I'd spent with my grandmother specifically her desire that I could follow in her footsteps.

I felt uncertain though. All my life until I came here, I never had any psychic or paranormal experiences. The only ghosts I had seen before were in movies. Maybe it had something to do with that house?—that whatever latent ability I had, was roused when I went there. I mentally scoffed. Yeah, GM had *nothing* to do with my burgeoning talents. Yeah. Riiiight. But she was so positive that I always had this ability...that she'd sensed it the day I was born.

And still, I only had a vague notion of the dangers involved. Who the hell were the 'enemies' GM referred to?

I drained the last of the latte and got to my feet. It was still too soon to make up my mind about all of this. Maybe the answer would become clear to me in a few days. It was time to go back and face the music. For sure, Lawrence would be pissed about my taking the car without permission. Well, screw him.

FOURTEEN

Lawrence was waiting at the top of the front steps when I drove in the driveway. He ambled down the stairs, his arms folded over his chest as he walked around the car, inspecting it. His lips were pursed as he looked over the shining surface for any scratch or dent.

I got out of the car and met him eye to eye. "The car's fine. I just needed to get out for a bit." My fingers rose high and I dangled the keys in front of his nose. "It's GM's car, right?"

His eyes narrowed and he snatched the keys from my hand. "She's awake now. She worried when I told her you had taken the car and gone off."

"Well, I'm back now." I tucked my purse strap higher on my shoulder and hummed a tune walking up the stairs. If he was expecting some sort of apology or explanation, he wasn't getting one from me. GM would understand when I talked to her. She was more in touch with the way she'd been at one time—carefree—than Lawrence ever was. He acted like he was born old.

Pushing open the slab of a front door I knew there was

plenty of time to take a quick shower and be dressed for cocktails with GM. With a bit of luck, my bedroom would be empty. I didn't need any more appearances from the other side...at least not today.

Heading up the staircase, my nostrils flared when I caught a whiff of what Lawrence was cooking. Yuck, ham! I hate ham for dinner. Yes, it's contrary—I love it in a sandwich, but not for dinner. I wondered if Lawrence knew this somehow. Sure wouldn't surprise me if he did. Talk about passive aggressive. I sighed; I'd just choke it down.

When I stepped up into my room and looked around, I breathed a sigh of relief. Everything was in order and my camera was still on the desk where I'd left it.

Forty minutes later, in a sleeveless cotton shirt dress, my hair styled and fresh make-up, I was ready for the next session with GM I paused on the stairway and considered that for a moment. Dressing for dinner? Cocktails first? Had I dropped into an episode of Downton Abby? I smiled and continued into the living room. I wondered what the old dame had in store for me this time.

GM was standing at the window, gazing out at the front yard. She turned when I entered. "You really must warn Lawrence before you take the car again, Keira. That Caddy is his pride and joy." Her gaze drifted to the floor for a moment and then she looked up at me. "Actually, why don't we get you your own car? It would be easier on dear Lawrence." Her chin rose and she grinned. "Something fast and sporty."

Was she trying to bribe me now? The house hadn't been enough that she thought giving me a car, NOW, would do the trick? "GM I still don't know if I'm taking you up on your offer. Buying a car for me...I don't know." I moved to the sideboard and poured two drinks from the silver canister. As I handed the glass to her, I grinned, "Maybe a rental would do."

She shook her head and patted my arm. "You remind me too much of myself, sometimes. We'll get Lawrence to take you in tomorrow to get you set up with a car." As we ambled to the sofa, she continued, "He'll make sure you get your bank card for the account I set up for you."

I stopped short and my mouth fell open as I stared at her.

She smiled. "It's not much. Just a couple of thousand. I trust if you take it into your head that you're going back to New York, you'll let me know first." She settled herself on the sofa, tucking the silk folds of her jacket into her lap.

OMG! I was completely beside myself as I sank onto the soft cushion on the other side of the sofa, looking at her. "That's very kind of you GM" A part of me knew that it was just one more piece of the grand design to keep me here to continue her work but still, considering my own parents had cast me off penniless, I was nevertheless floored.

"Nonsense. You need money to get around and besides..." She reached over and squeezed my knee. "You're family."

As I was about to take a sip from the drink, her hand rose to halt my arm. "Can you hold off on that just for a few minutes?"

My eyes narrowed and I set the glass on the coffee table. "Sure. Any particular reason?" She was up to something.

She laughed and brushed a hair from the black fabric of her pants. "Indulge me. I want you to sit back and close your eyes."

My eyebrow rose as I stared at her and settled into the upholstery. I took a deep breath and placed my hands on my lap and shut my eyes. The air was still and the only sound was the tinkling of her gold bangles on her wrists. The sweet scent of roses filled my nostrils again.

"I want you to picture your drink sitting on the coffee table. Get a clear image in your mind. Smell the sharp aroma, see the icy droplets on the sides."

My mouth watered at the thought of the tart, lime drink. I could taste it, feel the cool drink going down my throat. Underlying these thoughts was the question of why I was doing this.

"Focus, Keira."

Okay, okay. The glass, not its contents. I emptied my mind of everything but the glass. It pulsed and the outside became sharp in my mind.

"Picture the glass sliding across the table towards me." Her voice was soft and I could feel her gaze bore through me.

The glass. Moving slowly across the polished surface. I could feel my hands tighten together as I willed the glass to move.

"Relax your body. There is only the glass. It wants to move. Go with it. There is energy pushing on it. You just need to focus more pressure." Her words were barely a whisper.

It seemed like minutes had transpired before she spoke in a normal voice. "Open your eyes, Keira."

I jerked back when I saw where the glass was. It was half way across the table! I looked over at GM. Had she tricked me and moved it?

"I didn't move it, Keira. You did." Her gaze was soft and dreamy but her chin drooped lower. The fine lines crosshatching her cheeks were more pronounced the way she held her head.

"Are you sure? C'mon! I did that? Just by willing it to move?" I stared at the glass and for a moment my legs felt like strands of spaghetti...total mush, not even al dente. This was unbelievable. I sat back and blinked a few times, my brain totally fried.

"Yes. You willed the glass to move, capturing its energy and the energy around it with your mind." She looked over at me and smiled. "Not bad for your first time." She huffed a sigh. "My first time, the glass only moved an inch. I wasn't even sure it had moved."

My head turned and I looked at her wide-eyed. "You do this? I got this ability from you." It was a statement not a question. "Show me what you can do." I jerked my head indicating the chair across from us. "Can you move that chair?" I'd be seriously impressed if she could do that.

"Certainly. But I'm not going to." She leaned forward and handed me my drink. "You've earned it. Go ahead."

There was a pause and I swallowed half the glass in one gulp, waiting for her to continue. It tasted even better, knowing what I'd done!

She glanced over at me and then she spoke, "This isn't parlour games, Keira. I only practise telekinesis when I need to. For you...well, you're learning at this stage. It's my job to guide you. Practise on small objects and you'll become stronger. But be respectful of this power. Don't use it against people and don't use it frivolously, to show off."

I giggled. "Me? Show off? I'm taking this on the road, GM. I'll give David Copperfield a run for his money!"

She shook her head from side to side and sighed loudly. "What am I going to do with you, child? You are my Karma." She picked up her drink and took a long sip.

"Of course, you mean that in a good way, right?" Even I couldn't keep a straight face when I said that.

"Get me another drink. I need it with you around." But her eyes laughed when she looked at me, extending her glass.

I polished my gimlet off and licked my lips before popping up out of the chair. I spun around and looked at her. "Wait. Maybe I'll will the pitcher over here and get it to pour for us."

She reached out and her hand gave me a swat on the behind. "Get on with you, smartass!"

As I walked over, carrying our glasses, I pictured the Disney movie, Beauty and the Beast, the tea pot flying around and the dancing candelabras. I was living the dream. This was a talent I could have fun with, despite GM's warning.

***

When we took our seats at the table and Lawrence stood at the side board slicing the horrid ham, I was sorely tempted. Just a slight nudge at the back of his knees to make him falter...not fall, but just have to step quickly to keep his balance.

"Keira!" GM's mouth was set in a straight line and she glowered at me.

Damn! That was another trick I wanted to learn. Her ability to read minds. I spied the linen napkin next to my plate and closed my eyes. Picturing it lifting and settling on my lap. I sat there quietly concentrating for a minute before one eyelid crept open to peek. Only the corner of it had lifted and now rested on my plate.

"Patience. At this stage, having a clear mind is essential. I'm afraid that the gin isn't helping your cause." GM chuckled. By itself, her own napkin lifted, snapped with a flourish and then gently spread itself on her lap. She looked over at me and there was a twinkle in her eye.

I stuck out my tongue. "Show-off."

Still grinning, she shrugged. "Tomorrow, we'll do more exercises. After you get back from town and take me for a ride in your new car."

Lawrence was about to set the platter of ham garnished with golden pineapple on the table but he paused and his eyes were wide, staring at GM

"I hope that's okay with you, dear. I told Keira you'd take her to town and get her a car. I tried to talk her into purchasing one but she seems bent on renting." Her smile was sweet and innocent when she gazed up at him. "Oh, and she'll need to stop at the bank to get her card and do all that sort of thing."

"Pamela. Are you sure about this?" His eyes darted to me before looking back at her.

"Of course. Even if she decides to leave at some point, she'll need money and transportation. I know the Caddy is your baby." She cleared her throat and took the platter from his hand, effectively ending any argument on his part.

I could picture it now...a red Miata or a Ferrari. I could get used to this.

FIFTEEN

After GM went to bed, I tried my luck a few times at the telekinesis trick and failed miserably. I decided to get caught up on email and social media. For once, there was no ghostly activity and I didn't know whether to be happy about that or irritated. I had to pick up my own clothes and tidy up my room.

I sighed as I bent over to grab the blouse I wore last night and stopped cold. Wait a minute. I stood up and gave my head a shake. What the hell? Just a few days ago I was freaking out because of Molly's picking up after me. *Molly?* What the hell? A *freaking ghost* had been in my room! Of course I would freak out!

But now, standing there, holding the blouse I was irked because she's falling down on the job? What. The. Hell? In just a few days I had gone from a perfectly normal 24 year old to some weirdo who's comfortable with ghosts flitting in and out of her bedroom.

I couldn't help but laugh at myself as I tidied up.

I sent Mom a quick email, but got bored with everything

else. Honestly, Facebook, Snapchat and all the other stuff online paled in comparison to keeping the Universe safe, you know?

I shut off my computer and phone and climbed into bed. I cuddled under the covers and said out loud, "Goodnight Molly. Goodnight Sam."

It was the most peaceful night's sleep I had in quite some time.

**

The next morning I chose a short flared skirt and loose silk top for my trip into town to get the car and banking squared away. When I went down to the kitchen to rustle up some breakfast, Lawrence was sitting at the small table with his laptop open. I poured a glass of milk and popped a couple slices of bread into the toaster before turning to look over at him. I wasn't looking forward to the drive, alone in the car with the old goat but hopefully, I'd have my own wheels on the ride home.

"Hey Lawrence. What time do you want to go into town?" I leaned back against the counter and forced a smile.

For once, he managed to smile when he looked up. "Keira. Sometimes your grandmother forgets how simple life can be. I've called the bank manager and the car rental agency." He shifted the screen of the computer away from him and extended his hand. "All you need to do is pick out the car you want and I'll let them know which one to bring out. " He glanced at his watch. "The bank representative will be here with the paperwork and your card in fifteen minutes."

Holy cow! I almost choked on the milk I'd just taken a sip of. Lawrence was good. I could see why GM had kept him around so long. And better yet, we both avoided being in the Caddie together. I stepped over to the computer to see the selection of cars. There were sedans, four by fours and trucks. I scrolled down and then my eyes lit up.

"That's the one." I pointed to a fire engine red Miata.

He leaned over to see what I'd selected. "Are you sure

about that? I mean you could have a sporty jeep or something just a little sturdier. That one's a tin can for God's sake."

"Nope. That's the one." I spun around and tried to keep from skipping across the kitchen floor. The fact that he hated it; well, that just sealed the deal. My toast popped up and I busied myself buttering it and spreading marmalade, all the while eavesdropping as he placed the call.

I picked up the milk and the plate of toast and left the room. GM was probably in the sun room waiting for me. When I entered, she looked up from the book she was reading and plucked the glasses from the end of her nose.

"Well, don't you look nice today!" Her gaze took in the princess heeled sandals up my bare legs to my neckline. "I remember wearing skirts that short. Those were the days." She smiled and her fingers tugged the high collar of her blouse even higher on her crepe neck.

"Thanks. I dressed thinking I was going into town. But Lawrence has it all covered." I sat down and arranged the plate and milk before me. Again, the delicate aroma of roses seasoned the air in the room. GM must be wearing a scent, because I only notice that aroma when she's nearby.

She cut me off before I could ask her what brand of perfume she used. "He's such a wonder, that man! What would I ever do without him?" Her gaze became unfocused as she looked into her yesterdays and a small smile played across her lips.

I looked at her as I munched on the piece of toast. Although I couldn't share her affection for the old coot, he did something wonderful for GM. Had they ever...uh, done it? No. Erase that image right off my retinas. GM and Lawrence? No way. The toast was a lump going down my throat. Got to get my mind out of the gutter before I choked to death.

"What's on my training schedule for today, GM? Do you have a new way to scare the hell out of me or am I going to work on making dinner napkins float?" I blinked as coyly as I could. Which was, to be honest, pretty good. I had lots of practice with Dad. He always fell in line when I played the coy card.

"The coy card doesn't work on women, Keira; you know that." She winked at me and then her chin rose high, barely able to keep the corners of her lips from twitching.

I jerked forward. "That! I want to know how you do that GM! How do you know what I'm *thinking*? Now that's a skill I'd like." This could be seriously handy. I could go to the casino with Gwen and her Dad and play a poker. I'd clean out the table for sure. I'd give them the winnings since I didn't have any money worries...not anymore.

I paused and it hit me. That's a complete turnaround from hitchhiking back to New York. Was I seriously considering taking my grandmother's place now? I huffed a sigh. I was. Oh boy...

"It's a gift, not a 'skill', Keira. It develops in stages."

"What's the first stage then?"

She put her finger over her mouth considering for a moment. Then with a quick nod, said, "I suppose there's no time like the present." Leaning towards me, she said, "I'd like to see how you do with the banker and the car rental guy. When they arrive, I'll be at your side. It's common courtesy to shake hands and we'll both have the opportunity to do that. I'd like you to sense something personal about them."

"Okay! Is there some trick to this? Do I have to say some magic words or something?"

"No magic words nor spells, Keira. What you will need to do is clear your mind. With a clear mind you'll be more receptive to their thoughts. If you have the gift, their thoughts... well, at least their feelings, will come to you." She held up a finger. "But... especially at the beginning, you need to have a clear mind."

I blinked a few times hard, staring at her. "But I'll be too excited to clear my mind. With a new car and money of my own, how can I *not* think of that? Can we find someone else to do this with?" It wasn't fair. She knew how excited I was about the car.

"Relax. It's just the first attempt. And a car is just a car.

You'll own many over your life time. The important thing is you must begin to take your role seriously; and that begins with training." She leaned forward and covered my hand with hers. I could feel a pulsing sensation, a warm energy from her touch. As she held my eyes, she said with an intensity I never saw before, "I won't be here forever, Keira. You must learn now, while there's time."

It hit me like a wall. My eyes smarted and my throat grew tight. In one more second I'd be crying. "Don't talk like that, GM."

"Keira, it's the truth... I'm a very, very old woman. And this is important work."

"I know! I know! But... you're not...*really, really* sick, are you? I mean... you're not dying now, are you?" I was shocked at myself at how big a part of my heart this woman already occupied. I couldn't call her 'Nana' out loud just yet... but the idea of her being gone...the very idea of such a loss hit me like a wall.

She made a half assed attempt at a smile, and said, "No. I'm not *dying*."

I huffed out a burst of air. "Whew! You scared the hell out of me there, GM. More than Molly and Sam put together!" I tried to laugh lightly, and it came out like a cough. "Look, promise no more talk of you 'not being here' and I'll work on clearing my mind, okay?" I mustered up a weak smile. "Hell, when we take the car out for a spin, I'll even go the speed limit, alright?"

She chuckled and sat back, letting go of my hand. "Let's not go *too* crazy. Of course you'll go fast. The faster the better." Her hand rose and she tucked a stray lock of hair back into place. "One of my..." She cleared her throat. "...ahem, friends...used to say, if you're not living on the edge, you're taking up space."

I cocked an eyebrow at her. "A friend, huh?"

She gave me a coy smile. Coy. Her coy put my coy to shame. "A good friend, Keira. A very good and *very* handsome friend."

I closed my eyes and shook my head. This woman! "Okay. What do you want me to do to get ready for this?"

"Finish your milk and then sit back. You need to think of yourself as that empty glass. Nature hates a vacuum. When you've calmed yourself and feel that void, the energy of the next person you touch will spill into you." Her eyes were glazed and a little out of focus as she spoke. It was kind of like she was settling into the state of mind she'd described.

I set the glass down and then eased deeper into the chair's cushions, keeping my eye on the glass. I took a slow, deep breath and then closed my eyes, the glass still focal in my mind. As I exhaled I willed any thought or impulse out with the breath of air. I did this for the next eight breaths when the ringing doorbell broke my concentration.

My eyes popped open and I stared at GM She smiled and nodded her head. "It'll have to do, my dear. Lawrence will bring the bank person here."

I sat perfectly still, only slightly aware of the door closing and the muted sound of voices. As the footsteps neared, a woman's nasal voice became louder.

Lawrence appeared in the doorway and stood to the side, "Mrs. York, Edith Graham from your bank is here." He turned and as a blonde woman in her late thirties appeared, he continued, "This is Miss Swanson, who is the account holder."

The woman's grey eyes flitted to me and then settled on GM, moving sharply over with her manicured hand extended. "Pleased to meet you, Mrs. York."

GM gripped her hand lightly and nodded. She held the grasp for just a beat before glancing over to me.

Right on cue, the woman turned to me, bending slightly as she held her hand out before me. "Miss Swanson. So nice to meet you."

As soon as my flesh met hers, the image of a teen aged girl flashed in my mind. She was standing next to a brick wall, smoking a cigarette and laughing with a group of kids. Worry. That was the feeling that I sensed from the bank lady. Her eyes became questioning and she glanced at our hands before I released her.

GM's voice broke the silence. "Please have a seat, Mrs. Graham."

Lawrence moved to clear my dishes and the bank lady took a seat. She put a brown briefcase on the table and the next half hour was taken up with signatures and setting up the P.I.N. for my checking account.

When she finally left, GM turned to me. "Well?"

"She has a teenage daughter that she's worried about." I couldn't get the words out fast enough. I'd done it! I knew that I'd read it right. This was freaking amazing!

"Good work!" GM leaned forward and patted my arm. "She's right to be worried. That kid is hanging out with the wrong crowd. She's cutting classes and she's pregnant with some punk's kid. Poor Edith, consoles herself with a bottle of wine every night, which isn't helping the cause. She's trying, all on her own since that lazy husband left her. He doesn't even provide child support."

My mouth fell open, the wind totally out of my sail now. "How did you pick all *that* up?"

Her eyes rose to meet mine and she grinned. "Practise my dear. Years and years of practise." She slapped the table and rose to her feet. "Now! Let's go out to the front door. Your car is about to pull into the driveway." She gripped her cane and still grinning like the cat who'd swallowed the canary, she tottered out the door.

I was still smoked by all she'd picked up compared to my scant gleanings as I trailed her out of the room. The bell chimed again and Lawrence opened the door wide. Standing there was the most gorgeous hunk of male I'd seen in quite some time. He was about thirty, tall, swarthy complexion and the bluest eyes I'd even seen stared back at me. For a moment, I paused, ogling this Adonis, my heart beating hard against my rib cage. I was totally glad my skirt was short and I looked hot.

"Someone order a car?" His voice was smooth as creamy butter on a hot piece of toast. Ignoring Lawrence and GM he only had eyes for me.

"I do! I mean, I did!" I gulped. Oh Lord, I sounded like I was in High School. My face burning, I rushed forward, brushing past Lawrence and slithering by Mr. Hottie. I took my time with the slither.

There it was! The red caught the sun's rays, burnishing it like it was a flame. The top was down, showing two dark leather seats tucked behind a smoke tinted windshield. It was sleek and moulded with the headlights like eyes.

"Keira!" My grandmother's voice quietly admonished me, bringing me out of my ogling.

Surely she didn't expect me to be able to read the hot guy's thoughts! I mean...it would be too much! I was in love with the car and in lust with the guy! I turned and extended my hand. "I'm Keira. The car's for me."

His grip was warm and firm. "I'm Alex."

The flash in my mind made my cheeks get hotter still. He was picturing me naked. There was a king sized bed, wine and candles. My body tingled and I quickly withdrew my hand. It was a good thing he couldn't read MY thoughts!

GM had sidled up closer and she now gripped his hand, introducing herself while his eyes kept creeping over to where I stood. Her eyes widened a little and her chin rose higher.

"I'll need a credit card and your driver's license, Keira." Alex pulled his hand back and puzzlement was in the look he shot GM.

"Sure. It's... up in my bedroom." Our eyes locked, and I didn't need to be touching him to know what he was thinking.

"Keira." GM was being such a wet blanket.

My smile dropped and I rushed across the foyer, feeling Alex's eyes on my bare legs as I raced up the stairs. I was definitely getting his business card when I got back. Maybe I could give him a ride back to town. Maybe to his place? And maybe... I grabbed my purse out of my room and headed out of the room.

When I got back down an older, grey haired guy was standing next to GM She was just giving him back a clipboard and a pen. Where was Alex? My stomach fell as I walked forward.

"Hi Keira. I'm Phil Donovan. I came out here to run Alex back to the office. I'll just need your driver's licence and we're done here. You've got the car for as long as you want. Try not to get too many speeding tickets." He laughed as he took my driver's licence and began copying down the numbers. "It just came from the dealership yesterday, you know."

"So it's brand new?" I clapped my hands when he nodded. A brand new car!

Lawrence came up from the driveway where the car was parked. "I gave the car the once over. Not a scratch." His eyes narrowed when he glanced over at me. "Make sure it stays that way."

Phil handed me back the driver's license and car key before shaking my hand. It was brief and just a hint of his quick calculations on the money he would get from this deal flashed in my mind. "Have fun with the car!"

He turned to GM and then bounded down the stairs, and out to the driveway. A hand emerged from the driver's side window in the beige sedan and waved to me. I hadn't even got Alex's business card. I sighed.

GM's eyebrows were high and her eyes were flinty watching them leave. It was Alex. There was something about him that she didn't like. Again, no need to be a mind reader to judge by the puckered, tight lips in her face. "Well, that's that. Well? Are you taking me for a spin or not?"

I didn't have to be asked twice. I joined her and extended my elbow for her to hold as we walked down the steps.

"Take it easy, Keira!" Lawrence pointed his finger at me before ambling back inside and closing the door.

GM scoffed. "He worries too much! Just don't break the sound barrier my dear. I have my limits too." She smiled at me as I held the car door for her. I held her hand as she folded her body and plopped down on the seat. "My. This *is* low."

My stomach was doing cartwheels as I shut the door and hurried around the car to the driver's side. When I got inside, there was that sweet new car smell mingling with the leather.

"Here we go!" I turned the key in the ignition and orchestrated a four point turn till I was nudging out the end of the drive. The sun beat down on my head and a slight breeze lifted my hair.

Once we were on the main road, the acceleration, the motor purring like a kitten was liberating. The steering and handling were perfect, just the way I'd imagined. I sneaked a peak at GM and smiled. She'd put her seat belt on and her hand curled around the grip on the door, but her eyes were shining with excitement.

"So what was so wrong about Alex? I could tell you didn't like him." I glanced over at her before turning back to watch the road.

"Aside from his X rated thoughts, you mean? He sure wasn't thinking of his wife and three year old son." Her eyebrow rose high when her eyes met mine.

That jerk! His good looks and flirting seemed sleazy now. No wonder GM managed to get Phil to complete the transaction. Yuck! I was glad I didn't get his card and if he dared to call me on some pretext of following up... I'd ask how's the wife and kids!

I smiled seeing the straight stretch with not a car in sight. My foot pressed the accelerator and we leapt forward. There was quite a bit of pep to this car. I eased off and turned into a road going off to the right. GM's hair was a wild nest of feathery wisps around her face and she'd probably had enough.

On the way back, I remembered Gwen's invitation for later that day and slowed a little to watch for her blue mailbox. "Hey! You know your mail lady, Gwen?"

GM's gaze flitted to me and she nodded.

"I ran into her in town yesterday and we had coffee. She invited me to go for a swim in her pool later today." Even though I had the sharp set of wheels, I'd probably walk in case we had a few drinks. I scanned the mailboxes as we drove. It had to be not far from where we were now.

"I don't think that's such a good idea. You have work to do with me and—"

"I'm not going until after four, when you're having your nap." I looked over at her, surprised to see the scowl on her face, her eyes wide, staring at me.

"No, Keira; that's a bad idea."

What? "How is it a bad idea?"

"You have *work* to do. While I'm napping, I want you to see if you can contact Molly and Sam in your room. You also need to work on your telekinesis. " Before I could say a word, she added, "As far as making friends with the locals..." She shook her head emphatically. "No. I'm against this."

"You're against it."

"Yes. The nature of what we do, becoming friendly with people who live nearby only complicates things." She raised an eyebrow. "They start asking questions that you won't want to answer, prying into your business, and generally become a nuisance." She slapped the dashboard in front of her. "No. You have more important things to do with your time than some silly pool party. You need to cancel."

Cancel? First of all, even if I wanted to cancel, which I didn't, I didn't have her phone number to do that. And what was the big deal about a couple of hours away from the house? GM wouldn't even be awake during the time I was gone. "I'm going. I will be back for drinks and dinner, don't worry." I kept my voice even, despite GM's high and mighty attitude. *She's not the boss of me!*

GM was being quiet but from the puckered moue of her lips, she was angry. I didn't get it. How could something this trivial set her off like that? But, I wasn't giving in either. She couldn't expect me to be a recluse. And I'd hardly call a two hour swim with Gwen, *a party.*

I parked the car next to the Caddie and turned it off. My shoulders slumped for a moment as I sat there. She'd been so generous and this had certainly put a damper on the festive mood from earlier. I guess there was always a catch.

I got out and walked around the car to get GM's door for her. If she wasn't so angry, it would have been comical, seeing her hair, a cotton candy mess framing her flushed cheeks and flinty eyes. But I knew better than to make any smart ass comment. Instead, I tried one more time, "Look, I'm sorry you feel that way about me going over to Gwen's. I thought you liked her. I'll make sure I'm back in time for drinks."

She gripped my arm and set the point of her cane on the ground, pushing and pulling her frail frame up from the seat of the car. "Make sure you are, then." When she got to her feet she gazed solemnly into my eyes. "I told you earlier, this is not a game, Keira. You need to learn a lot of things if you are to do this work. Don't disappoint me."

SIXTEEN

Her words hit me like a kick to the stomach. I felt like I was twelve years old and had just gotten a scolding. GM's rant was too much like something my parents would say to me. I could see the disappointment in me in her eyes. All my efforts: social work, photography and last but not least the acting school debacle hung around my neck like an albatross. I felt like such a loser as I escorted her up the stairs.

Lawrence was waiting, holding open the front door. Great.

Maybe I'm flighty. Or maybe like Gwen said, I haven't found my passion yet. It didn't matter. One quality I do have is I *am* stubborn. And I was going swimming that afternoon, one way or another; so there.

"Lawrence, Keira and I will be in the living room. Would you mind bringing us lunch there in an hour? In the meantime, we'll need a pot of tea." At least she hadn't said anything about my visit with Gwen.

His eyes flicked to me. "In the living room? Not the sun room?"

"That's correct, dear."

"And, I suppose, you want the House Blend, not Earl Grey." He ran his hand through his hair. "Shall I be joining you then?" he asked quietly.

She nodded sagely.

"You're sure about this?"

"Yes."

"Very well." He turned and headed to the kitchen.

Before I could ask what that was all about, she turned to me and her voice was business-like, rather than her normal, light tone. "Keira, make yourself comfortable and I'll join you in a few minutes. I need to tidy my hair." With that she turned and her cane keep a steady beat as she walked down the hallway to her bedroom and bath.

I set the car keys on the small table near the door and ambled into the living room. I flopped down into the sofa and crossed my legs, feeling a lot like so many other times when I'd skipped school or been busted for some infraction, waiting in the principal's office. I took a deep breath and shook my head from side to side. This was stupid. GM might be miffed about me going to Gwen's but she'd get over it.

Whatever she wanted to teach me this session, I'd concentrate on learning. She'd see that she was being unreasonable and that I was up to the mark. Even though I still wasn't one hundred percent convinced I was staying, at least I'd give it the old college try.

There was a small vase of pink rosebuds on the table in front of me. Perhaps if she came in and saw me practising my telekinesis she'd recant her earlier words. I sat back and made myself comfortable, breathing slow and steady as I focused on the vase of flowers. My eyes closed and I envisioned the energy surrounding it...saw it draw together and push the vase.

The soft hiss of the glass moving over the surface drifted into my ears. It was working! I kept focusing, even more this time, willing more energy. It seemed like a long time before the swishing sound stopped. And then...

The sharp sound of shattering glass startled me. My eyes flew open and there was the vase in a million pieces, the roses in a pile amid the spreading water on the floor around it. Damn it; this day just kept getting better and better. I scrambled forward and then got up to run for some towels to mop the water up.

Just as I reached the doorway, there was GM, her hands tucked up the sleeves of her loose jacket, staring at me silently.

"I'm sorry. I was practising and it went too fast...I mean, the vase went too far. I'll clean it up." I stammered under her reproving gaze at me and then the floor where the glass shards sat. I raced across the foyer and into the kitchen. Lawrence looked up from where he was pouring hot water into a china tea pot. "I broke her vase." I spotted the roll of paper towels on the counter and grabbed it.

When I got back, GM was perched on the chair across from the sofa, her hands on the head of the cane, looking away from me.

"I'll just be a minute." I bent and spread the towel, taking care of the pieces of glass and wiped up the mess. I scooped everything in my hands and walked quickly back to the kitchen to deposit the debris in the garbage can.

"The tea is ready. I'll follow you in." He picked up the tray and nodded with his head for me to precede him.

My cheeks flamed as I walked back into the room. One of my first forays on my own with telekinesis and I'd managed to smash a crystal vase. I could almost feel the smug look on Lawrence's face as he followed me into the room. I took a seat across from GM and watched him pour tea into three cups. He was joining us. That was a first.

GM smiled up at him. "Thank you, dear." She turned to me, while out of the corner of my eye, I noticed Lawrence taking his tea to a chair near the door. "It's time you learned first-hand about transitioning. Lawrence is always close by when I do this. I learned the hard way, many years ago how important it is to have someone with his gifts nearby."

I looked over at Lawrence. He was about to take a sip of tea but his hand paused mid-air before his smiling lips. "More skill than gifts, Pamela. You ladies have gifts, not I."

"I won't argue semantics Lawrence." She turned back to me. "Occasionally, during a transition, other... powers try to interfere."

This didn't sound good. "Powers? What sort of powers?"

Lawrence spoke up from his vantage point. "Dark forces, Keira." He tried to look casual, sitting there sipping tea, but I saw he was alert by how he was leaning forward. "There are powers that do not want the spirits to transition. They crave the havoc that ensues."

"GM said something about them to me."

"Good." He looked to GM and asked, "Did you tell her how you become vulnerable during these transitions?"

Before GM could say a word, I held up my hands. "Wait a minute. Vulnerable? Vulnerable to what?"

His eyes flitted back to me, while his face was still on GM. "Attacks. That's why I'm here. When your Grandmother is communing with those poor, misbegotten souls, she's unable to sense impending evil." He pointed a finger to his chest. "I, on the other hand, am able to sense it coming. It's nothing paranormal, though; it's just a change in the... 'atmosphere' of the room. Pamela's too engrossed with her work to pick up on it, but I'm able to."

Oh boy. "Attacks?" I didn't give a damn that my voice squeaked. "What happens?"

"Nothing, now that Lawrence is here, dear. He gets my attention, and in so doing, disrupts the ritual, and everything goes back to normal." GM saw that this was scaring me, and her voice took on her gentle tone again.

"But what if he's unable to? He senses trouble coming—has he ever *not* been able to... stop it?" My eyes went from GM to Lawrence and back. "Just how much danger is there?"

GM crossed her arms. "I won't lie to you, Keira. To be honest, I didn't expect you to be so insightful so quickly and be asking these types of questions this soon."

"Yeah; I'm smarter than you gave me credit for. Thanks for that."

Now it was GM's turn to look abashed. She dropped her

head for a moment. "Yes, you're right. This home is the safest location for you to experience the... wonder of watching a spirit cross over."

"That's good to know, GM." I leaned forward and touched her shoulder. She felt frail. "But you didn't answer my question. Just how dangerous can this get?"

Her head rose sharply. "Very."

We stared at each other in silence. Honestly, I wasn't all that surprised. Just the other day we were discussing how the fabric of the Universe depends on this work, and how there exists an... an *evil* that is the Yang to GM's Yin and wants everything to go to shit. I took a deep breath. "*Really* very?"

She nodded. Damn.

"But you've been able to deal with it, right?"

She glanced over at Lawrence. "With help, but yes."

I looked over from her to him and back again. "Well, I guess that's good enough for now. I hope."

GM was silent for a long space, sipping her tea quietly weighing her words. "Before we start, there is something I need to give you." She reached in a hidden pocket of her pants and extended her hand to me. In her open palm was a black stone. "This is tourmaline. It possesses protective qualities."

I took the black stone from her and closed my fingers around it. It was smooth, warm and surprisingly heavy considering it was only the size of a grape. Aside from that, I didn't notice anything special about it.

"Close your eyes and take three breaths. Inhale to a count of four and exhale to a count of four. As you inhale, picture a pure white energy field that is coming into your body. On the exhalation, bid negative thoughts and feelings to leave."

Believe it or not, it was harder to do than it sounds. On the first inhale/exhale, I couldn't envision white energy; instead the image of a cascading waterfall was all I could come up with. I scrunched my closed eyes on the second breath, really trying to see a white curtain. By the time I did the third breath, I had it in my mind's eye and settled into the ritual. I opened my eyes, blinking a couple of times. Actually, I did feel a little calmer.

"Now we'll begin. Keira, finish your tea."

I sipped the tea, which had a pungent, minty flavour that lingered on my tongue. I shot a look over to Lawrence. "House Blend?" I asked.

He stayed silent, and GM answered. "Yes. It's a sacred blend that I try to drink before any of these rites."

"Where's it from?"

"California. Now finish it please, so we can begin."

I took a series of sips. Before I'd even finished, a feeling of calmness settled deeper in my body. I set the empty cup back in the saucer and put it on the tray.

"Alright, Keira. Let's begin."

I gazed at GM and took a deep breath. I was about to witness what she'd spent her life accomplishing...what she wanted me to carry on after her. Her hands sat loose, palms up on her knees and her chin rose.

"Mary Grace Clayburn, I summon you to appear to me." Her voice was low and commanding.

My gaze flitted over the room, specifically to the doorway. I'd experienced Molly, upstairs, not down in the living room. The air changed. It became cooler and somehow thicker on my skin.

As soon as I sensed the air change, I saw her begin to appear. At first it was a pinpoint of light that floated from the other side of the room towards GM. Gradually, it became bigger, the air around it shimmering, bending the shapes of the furniture it passed by. The orb morphed wider and a face began to appear. Her hair was dark, pulled up and back. Next, a long grey dress came into view. From the style and length, it was clear that it was from another period, long ago.

I didn't dare to breathe, sitting mesmerized by the apparition. I was actually seeing her! My grandmother had summoned her and she'd come! It was nothing short of awesome! I glanced past her, around the room, checking for any of these other 'entities' that GM and Lawrence had talked about...but there was nothing but the tremulous hazy image of

Molly.

"Mary Clayburn, it is time for you to leave this realm."

The apparition's eyes went wider and she shook her head from side to side. It was hard to tell if the expression was sorrow or fear.

But GM must have known, because she continued. "There is nothing for you here, Mary. You must go on. Follow the path that you were meant to travel and leave this earthly plane. Your home is beyond The Veil."

Mary's hands went up to cover her face and she shook her head 'no', even harder. The feeling of sorrow emanated into my body, coming off her in shimmering waves of grief. There was also confusion. As I stared at her, something inside me broke and tears began to flow. She was like a rabbit caught in the headlights of a car, frozen, not knowing where to turn.

I didn't dare to open my mouth, so I began to repeat the phrase '*Leave. You'll be happier*' silently. It became a mantra in my mind, repeating over and over as I gazed at her.

Then a curtain, the folds glittering with shining threads of silver and rose tinted hues appeared. They were gently billowing as if a breeze was behind it, parting The Veil to reveal a glare of light, bright as the sun on a summer day. GM's voice was a whisper as she sat forward in her chair. "It's there, Mary. Go through to the other side. Lloyd, Tim and Alice are waiting for you. Join them."

"Lloyd." Although she'd mouthed the word, I could hear it in my mind, her voice a sweet soprano. She turned and stepped, or rather glided smoothly closer to it. Her hand rose and then disappeared into the light. She never looked back, when she took the next step and was gone.

"Samuel John Goodrich, I command you to appear."

I jerked and stared at my grandmother. As easy as that she'd got Molly to leave and was on to the next one! She smiled over at me. "Keira, would you like to try it?" When my mouth fell open, she continued. "I'm here to help, don't worry. He's talked to you, so that will help."

I sat forward and waited silently for Sam to make himself

known. Maybe I needed to run upstairs and get my camera. He'd liked playing with it, the little bugger. "Sam? Please come to us." My voice was tentative. Would he appear?

A thud came from the stairs followed by three more. I jumped in my seat and then spun to peer at the doorway, where the noise had originated. A red and blue rubber ball rolled in from the hall and across the floor, coming to a standstill at my foot. The air began to warp and shimmer and his shape took form. It was the same little boy, I'd encountered in my room. The same striped shirt, the jeans and the tow blonde hair that went everywhere but flat on his head. But his face was blank, like he was totally surprised to be there. He looked around the room and then his wide eyed gaze turned to me.

The poor child was terrified.

"Sam? Don't be afraid. I want to help you, not hurt you." It was no wonder he was frightened. He'd been kept a prisoner in the attic and when he was finally free of it, he'd landed in the twenty-first century. It would be like setting foot on Mars. I gazed into his eyes, feeling my own well with fresh tears. To be so young and die without the freedom of ever being outside, playing in the sun. Whatever was on the other side of that curtain *had* to be better than what he was going through right then.

I left my seat and approached him. I know I should have been frightened, but I wasn't, not the slightest.

"You're free now Sam. You can leave." I glanced to where The Veil still shimmered and gently wafted. "It's there, Sam. Go through now."

His eyes spanned wide. "No! I'm not allowed to leave. You don't understand!" His hand streaked out and icy fingers grasped mine. "I'll be good! Just let me stay!"

Tears burned my eyes and my hand curled tighter on his. "You *are* a good boy. That's why you have to leave. You deserve more than this. There's no place for you here. Your family is behind that curtain, waiting for you."

It was exactly the *wrong* thing to say. His head shook from side to side and there was abject terror on his face. His hands tore at my arms, clinging to me, making my skin almost freeze.

GM was on her feet extending her hand to rest on his shoulder. "Sam. They can't hurt you anymore. Your favourite sister, Irene, is over there. She wants to play tag with you." She grasped his hand and pulled it away from my arm. "Come. I'll hold your hand. I won't let go until you do. Okay?"

He looked up at her, his eyes full of trust even though from the way he slowly left my side, there was still some fear. GM stopped just short of the waving folds of the curtain and nodded to him, urging him forward. His eyes lingered on hers before he turned and peeked beyond The Veil. A smile blossomed on his lips. I couldn't see what he saw but whatever it was, it must have been good. His hand dropped from GM's and he stepped through.

He, along with the glittering curtain were gone in the blink of an eye.

Immediately, Lawrence was at my grandmother's side, his arm circling her waist, helping her back to the chair. "Pamela, you *must* rest now." When she was seated, he straightened and glanced over at me. "How are you doing, Keira?"

I couldn't tell whether the transition thing or Lawrence showing genuine care about my well being was more of a shock. I swiped the tears that had dribbled onto my cheeks away, taking stock of how I felt. I was tired, like I'd run a marathon but my mind was still in the race. It had been an awesome experience. I had a million questions to ask them! Yes, them. Lawrence had been a part of it, even if just sitting the sidelines making sure things didn't go off the rails.

"I'm fine...a little tired but I'll be over that in no time, I'm sure." I slipped the black stone into my pocket. A little tired? I flopped into my seat.

He laughed. "Pamela usually has a glass of orange juice and slice of key lime pie after a session. Would you like some?"

My mouth watered. Suddenly, I realized I was ravenous. To hell with the calories! Pie and orange juice were just what the doctor ordered! "Perfect! Can I have a double slice?"

GM chuckled. "Sure beats melon and marshmallows, don't it?" She leaned over and patted my knee. "We can eat *healthy* tonight. You did well, Keira."

Lawrence's hand squeezed GM's shoulder and she gazed up at him, her own hand covering his. "Thanks, dear. What would I do without you?"

He smiled. "You'll never have to know, Pamela." He moved off, walking towards the door. "Good thing I defrosted the pie."

When he left the room, I sat back. "So Molly and Sam are really gone?" I'd miss Molly, and well...Sam, his story just had to get better after he left the house.

She nodded. "Sorry, no more maid service for you. But Sam...it was touch and go with him." Her hands gripped her knees and she stretched a little looking down at the floor. Under her eyes grape shaded cusps gave a hint that this had taken more out of her than she would admit.

"What would have happened if he chose to stay? I mean, you can't force him to leave, can you?" I looked down at my foot where the striped ball still lay and bent to pick it up. I'd keep this as a souvenir to remember my first time.

"I would never dream of it. No, it's important that a spirit leaves of their own accord. It's respecting their free will." She huffed a sigh. "In the end, they both chose and they are where they should be."

"With a little nudge from us."

She nodded, then glanced around the room. "And no interference...this time." She was silent for a few beats, watching me. "I know you're a bit drained right now...but inside, how did you feel when this was happening?"

As I returned her gaze, I could tell that this was the crux of the matter. I didn't have to think it over at all. "I have never felt so *right* doing something," I said softly. "I did something that really, really mattered." Our eyes held. I understood GM a hell of a lot better now. I could see how a person could make this their life's work.

She sat back in her chair when Lawrence walked in with

another tray of drinks and pie. "More importantly, as you'll come to see the more embedded in this you become...it was the right thing to do to keep the lines straight within the universe."

Yeah. But. I just dove right in. "You've had Lawrence with you when you've done this...the transitioning. But what about me? If I'm to do this after...after you're gone, won't I need someone like him, to kind of watch over me?" I didn't know how bad, bad could get but the very fact that Lawrence still insisted on being with GM when she did this, spoke volumes.

"You will. You will find that person or like me and Lawrence, that person will find you. Until that happen, don't be like me. Be cautious and know when to step away from a transition if you get a bad feeling." She took the glass of juice from Lawrence and smiled looking up at him.

"Or you could end up on your ass, clinging to a diving board high above the water." Lawrence grinned at her.

She held her hand up like a traffic cup! "Don't you dare say a word about the bathing suit."

He reached for my glass of juice to hand it to me. Under his breath, barely audible "What bathing suit?" He smirked at her as I took the glass from his hand.

Too much information. We'd cover this another time when Lawrence wasn't around.

SEVENTEEN

Walking down the shoulder of the two lane road towards Gwen's, I felt a weight lift from me. That experience with GM and the spirits was the most intense incident of my entire life, and I needed to catch my breath. At the age of 23, there was nothing I had ever been a part of that came close to what just happened.

I'm afraid of heights, okay? So, when I turned 21 I decided to take that bull by the horns and go skydiving. It was the most terrifying and exhilarating thing I had ever done. I freefell for about five seconds (that felt like about a half hour) before the parachute snapped open and I drifted down to earth. When my feet touched the ground, my knees went weak and I fell over. I laid on my side for a minute or so basking in the hugeness of what I had accomplished. When I got to my feet—the world was different somehow. *I* was different.

Well, jumping out of a plane a mile up in the air is *nothing* compared to what I was part of back at GM's house. Not one, but two ghosts appearing in the living room, that Veil... that beautiful and amazing portal just showing up, the blinding but somehow comforting light pouring through, and then 'poof' everything back to normal... It all happened so quickly, and yet it all felt somehow so natural... I had to step away from this and just let it settle in.

When GM headed in for her nap early, I told her I was going. She didn't get huffy with me. She just nodded. I could tell she wasn't crazy about the idea, but I think some of the division between us over my making friends with Gwen was healed by how I handled Molly's and Sam's transitions.

I came to a halt in my walk to Gwen's and turned my face up towards the sun. Its warmth bathed me. The disconnect of the afternoon hit me again. I had just had a glimpse of the hereafter and eternity when I saw the light emanating from behind The Veil, and here I was basking in the warm rays of the sun on my way to a dip in a swimming pool.

Well, I guess, life does go on, doesn't it?

It was just another minute or two before I turned up her driveway. I pulled the bag containing my swimsuit and towel higher on my shoulder. I hadn't gone swimming at someone's home in a long, long time. There's not a lot of houses with swimming pools in Manhattan, okay? Maybe I should have brought along a bottle of wine or something.

Yeah, life goes on.

I climbed the few steps and strode across the veranda and knocked on the door. It opened and Gwen stood there, wearing a bathing suit top and a pair of cut-off jean shorts. "Hi Keira! C'mon in." Once again her hair was tied back in a pony tail that swished over her shoulders when she turned. Her arms were lean but the muscles were clearly defined; carrying mailbags must be a good workout.

"Hi Gwen." I stepped into the hallway. "Thanks for the invitation; it sure is a hot one today." It was cooler inside, but not by much.

"Tell me about it," she nodded. "The sweat was pouring off of me by the time I got off work." She nodded towards the living room. "Let me introduce you to my Dad."

We stepped into the room, and Gwen said, "Dad, this is

Keira. Keira, my Dad, Devon Jones."

Devon was older than my own father, probably in his 60's. He was completely bald and ensconced in an overstuffed wing chair at one end of the room. Like a lord of the manor, he had a Golden Lab curled at his feet and a ball game on the TV mounted on the opposite wall.

Except this lord of the manor also had a walker and cane set up beside his throne.

As I strode across the room with my hand outstretched, the dog scrambled to its feet and skulked around the chair putting it between us. I stopped and sighed. Why were dogs always freaked out when they saw me? I love dogs! Well... from afar, anyway.

Devon glanced over at the dog and back to me. "Some guard dog, huh?" he said with a faltering smile and held out his hand. When I stepped forward to shake it, the dog let out a low whine.

When I took Devon's hand in mine, a sad billow of forsaken loneliness washed over me, even though his face was smiling in welcome. His wife had been gone for years and he missed her still. Her tinkling laughter, her warmth in his bed, her cooking, and how she loved having company. It was all there at once in my mind, and complete.

"Pleased to meet you, Mr. Jones."

"Nice to meet you too, Keira." He had his smile back in place. "So you're Mrs. York's granddaughter?" He glanced up at Gwen and then turned back to me. "From New York? I was there only once, back in the eighties. How are you enjoying Kingston?" He pulled his hand back and rested it on the arm of the chair.

From the corner of my eye, I noticed Gwen rounding the sofa, patting her hand against her thigh, "What's wrong, Buster? C'mere." The dog let out another whine and slinked over to her.

I focused on Gwen's dad. "Good, although I haven't seen all that much of the city yet. My grandmother...well, I'm trying to spend most of my time with her." Another part of my mind was skipping lightly. I'd been able to sense his emotions and the sadness even though I hadn't consciously tried. I wasn't even in my grandmother's house and this had happened! The dog...well, I was used to them cowering away from me.

I glanced over at Gwen and right on cue she piped up. "We're having a swim and some beers, although not necessarily in that order. Would you care for a beer, Dad?"

"I'm fine right now." He looked down at his lap for a moment. "You two go on and enjoy your swim. I'll keep Buster company. Where did he get to?"

"He's hiding behind the sofa. I don't know what's up with him being *shy*." Gwen shrugged and her gaze flitted to me. "Normally he'd knock you over trying to lick your face."

"That's okay. Dogs don't take to me."

"They don't like you?" Devon asked.

"No... it's not they don't like me..." I gestured to where Buster was cowering. They're scared of me on sight." I shrugged. "It's kind of sad, actually, because I always wanted one growing up."

Gwen tilted her head. "That is a little odd; I've never heard of that. I've heard of dogs hating people on sight, but never being afraid of people on sight."

Devon eyed me up and down. "It's not like you're scary looking or anything. You look pretty normal to me."

If only you knew, Mister Jones, I thought to myself. Me and my grandmother are pretty, pretty far from normal. Instead, I just shrugged. "That's just the way it's been all my life."

"Well, you never have to worry about getting rabies from one then," Devon quipped.

I let out a laugh. "My own father said the same thing to me years ago."

"Smart man."

Gwen stood up from the sofa. "We'll just be out back so if you need anything, just holler." She nodded her head to the side and started across the floor. "The bathroom's just down the hall, Keira, if you want to get changed into your suit. I'll wait for you in the kitchen."

"Sure." I continued along to where she'd indicated, my footsteps making the floorboards creak in a few spots. The place was old but tidy. Handrails had been mounted to the wall of the hallway though.

In the bathroom again there were signs that things weren't easy for them. There were grab bars mounted beside the toilet and also in the bathtub. Inside the tub was a stainless steel stool and a shower wand. I quickly shucked my clothes and scrambled into my bathing suit.

When I walked into the kitchen, Gwen was leaning against the counter, a beer in her hand and towel draped over her neck. "Ready? I hope you drink beer. If you'd rather, I have wine too."

I walked over and lifted the icy bottle of beer. "Beer's fine."

"Good." She started for the door out to the pool, speaking over her shoulder. "So what'd you do today? Anything fun?"

As I followed her out, gazing to the sparkling blue pool a few feet away, I considered what to tell her. Certainly not the truth, *that* was for sure! "Oh! GM got me a car. It's a red Miata. It's got just the sweetest ride."

She turned and her eyebrows were high. "Just like that? She bought you a *car*?" She shook her head.

"It's just a rental. Something to get around while I'm here. Seriously, I've got to take you for a ride in it."

"A Miata." She stepped right up to me, and looked down. She had to be four, maybe six inches taller than me. "Think I'd fit?" she giggled.

I shot her a cheese grin. "Well, if not, we can strap you to the luggage rack on the trunk."

She snorted and we both flopped onto the lounge chairs.

"So how'd you make out at the casino with your dad? He seems like a pretty nice guy, by the way." I took a long pull at my beer and my eyes opened wider. This was some strong stuff! Way heavier taste than what I had back home. I glanced at the bottle.

"He is. But then again, I'm kind of biased. He was only down a few bucks when we left, which is a banner night in my books." She drank slowly and then wiped her lips with the back of her hand.

"Oh yeah? Maybe the next time, I'll join you. I could be your lucky charm." With how fast my talents have been growing under GM's tutelage, I'd probably be ready for the poker table before long.

"Yeah, sure." She took another pull on her beer and looked at me silently for a couple of seconds, like she was deliberating on something and then she spoke. "You know...in all the time I've been doing my job with the mail, I've only seen your grandmother and Lawrence a few times. They sure are loners. The only time I've seen a visitor there, is some woman who comes up every so often. She answered the door once, when I left a parcel."

"Did she have blonde hair, about my height?"

"Yeah, come to think of it she did."

"That was my mother."

"How come you never visited with her before this?" Gwen cupped her beer in two hands, her thumbnail toying with the label.

"I was busy with school, I guess." But seeing the look of disbelief in her eyes, I knew how weak that sounded. "Actually, to be honest, I never knew she even existed until recently."

"That's odd. Why would your mother keep that from you? I knew *my* grandparents for just a short while before they passed on, but even so I still remember them fondly."

I looked down at the edge of the pool for a few seconds. There wasn't much I could add that wouldn't give away the family secrets. I decided to steer away from this subject. "How about your mom? When did she pass away?"

Gwen's gaze fell. "Eight years ago. A brain tumour." A smile flitted across her face. "I swear there are times when I can feel her presence." She looked at me with a strange expression.

"Oh? How so?"

"This sounds crazy. But it's happened a few times. I'd be mooning around the house thinking of her, missing her like mad, and then her favorite song would come on the radio."

I shrugged. "Just coincidence, maybe?"

Gwen scoffed. "Yeah, I thought so the first time. I mean, I was trained as a scientist, right? But when it happened again, I started wondering."

"Go on..." She was onto something and now I was curious.

Gwen looked aside for a moment, and stared off. "It happens twice a year. On July 14th, at 10:30 am, and October 12th at 3:45 in the afternoon."

"You sound pretty sure about those days and times."

She nodded. "Those dates and times are when I miss her the most." She turned her head back to me. "My mother was born on July 14th at 10:30 in the morning." She held my eyes, and continued. "And she died at 3:45 in the afternoon on October 12th."

"Whoaaaa."

"Yeah, 'Whoaaa'. And it's the same song each time. *Snowbird* by Ann Murray." Gwen held my eyes. "Yeah, so my house is haunted; just like your grandmother's."

I blinked a couple of times. "What?"

"Your grandmother's house has a reputation for being haunted since I was a kid."

"Really?"

She nodded. "When I was growing up, kids would dare each other to go there on Halloween. We all thought it was haunted."

I picked at the label on the dark bottle for a beat or two. How much could I tell her without her thinking that I was part of the 'Addam's Family'? I looked over at her. "I can see that. I mean, it's old and kind of creepy looking, even though it's kind of a mansion. But I'm not sure it's all that scary when you live there." Vague, but at least I didn't out and out lie.

"What's really going on over at that house, Keira?"

I put my bottle on the table between us and sighed. GM was right about staying away from the locals. "Okay, I get it now. You're trying to pump me for gossip." I started to get up.

"Hey! No! Wait!" Gwen held out her hands. "Do you think

I've ever told *anyone* about my mother's song on the radio? I'm not looking for gossip, Keira!"

I kept my voice level. "Then what are you looking for?"

She sighed. "Data." She looked away, then back at me. "No. Not data. Information."

"Oh! I see! You need a ghost story! Okay!" Before she could stop me I said, "How about this one?" I waggled my eyebrows at her like a circus clown smoking crack. "Well... I've run into two ghosts, in my room. The first one, Molly—she's a clean freak picking up after me—and the second one is a little boy, Sam. He thinks his mother is coming to get him. He also likes playing with my camera. So far, that's about it!" I smiled brightly. Well, truth's stranger than fiction, right?

Gwen ran her hand over her head. "You know something? I think you just told me the truth, you know that? You're trying to make it sound like a bullshit story, but it's not, is it?"

I kept my mouth closed, watching the wheels turn behind her eyes.

She nodded. "Yep. You just told me the truth. Molly and Sam really happened." She nodded briskly. "I knew it."

"Why are you so sure?"

"Because of the light I saw one night at your grandmother's house, and because of the rose."

"What are you talking about now?"

"One night, not very long ago actually, I was taking Buster out for a walk. And when I went past your grandmother's home, I saw an incredible light shining out of the front windows. I never saw anything like it in my life. It was as bright as the sun; as if they were filming a movie inside there or something." Her eyebrows furrowed. "But it was different than light you see... it... I don't know how to describe it, it was *purer* or something."

I kept silent.

"Now I only saw that the one time." She held up her finger. "But. There's something very, very strange about your grandmother's garden."

"Oh?" God this girl was good. "What about her garden?"

"Her front yard has a little wall circling a bed of flowers. I've seen her tending the roses there." She looked off over to the end of the yard where a small garden shed stood.

"Yeah. Like I said, she loves her roses. What's weird about that?"

"There's one rose that blooms in the winter. Surrounded by a foot of snow but that rose still blooms."

I adjusted the strap of my bathing suit and cleared my throat. Anything to buy time before I answered. What could I say? There was no wiggling out of this one. "I don't know about that. Sure, I've seen the rose you're talking about but..." I shrugged my shoulders, kind of wishing I'd listened to my grandmother and cancelled this visit.

She continued, "At first I thought it was a silk rose but one day I got out of my truck and felt it; it was definitely real." Her dark eyes examined me like a bug under a microscope.

Time to give it up. She had me. I blew out a puff of air. "Yeah, it's real. What can I say? It's a strange house. I don't know why the rose blooms in winter but I've no doubt you've seen it." I grinned at her. "You haven't lied to me before."

She laughed. "Not that you know of."

I grinned at her like a wolf. "Wanna bet? Take my hand and I'll know." I thrust my hand out and grinned watching the puzzled smile on her face. I had never touched Gwen before, and was curious to see what I was going to come up with.

"Okaaaay?" She took my hand in hers and gave it a little shake. When she looked back up into my eyes she gasped.

The weirdest feeling came over me. I had just met her and now I knew...no, I *felt* everything about her. It came in a rolling cascade—her resentment of her older brother growing up, the worry and then pain of losing her mother, her genuine concern and love for her dad. It ended with a flash of her in safety goggles, her hands clutching a piece of green glass.

I pulled my hand back and deliberated for all of one second on whether to freak her out. "You do stained glass?"

Her jaw fell, staring at me. "I just started! I've taken some classes and now I'm working on a window hanging! How did you know?"

I fluttered my fingers in front of my face and in my most dramatic voice, "Madam Keira knows all." Her eyes were as big as golf balls peering at me. It was too much. I burst out laughing.

She leaned closer peering at me. "Your eyes when you took my hand...they changed. They got all kind of glassy...no they glittered. Seriously. That was weird. Your eyes got *strange!*"

I shrugged and looked off into the distance. It was still unsettling how quickly all that had happened. Whatever talents I had were coming to the surface faster and faster.

Gwen reached for my hand again. "Tell me more. Do it again. I mean how'd you do that? Are you some kind of—"

"No. Look it's been a day." When I saw the disappointment in her eyes, my tone grew softer. "I need you to drop it...for now. I'll explain at some point but, right now, let's just talk about something else." That same feeling of exhaustion I felt after transitioning Molly and Sam flowed over me again. I was beat.

She nodded. "Okay...but I'm going to hold you to that, you know. Talk about your Stephen King moment..."

"Does it frighten you?" I looked down at my fingers knotted together. I hoped it didn't scare her.

"What? No! You kidding? It's fascinating!"

"Really? It doesn't scare you?"

She shook her head. "I'm as surprised as you are. I *love* reading spooky stuff and watching scary movies. But this is... *real.*" She shrugged. "I have a scientific background, and a phenomenon like this is extraordinary! I'm more excited and curious than scared, Keira."

I lifted my head and looked at her again. When our eyes met, a flash of the two of us burst in my mind. We were older, in our thirties, waiting for a plane at an airport, We stood at the floor to ceiling windows, watching planes taxi off the tarmac. We were on our way somewhere, together. I gasped.

"Your eyes...for a moment there, they changed again, Keira."

I bet they did. I slowly got to my feet. "I'm not up for swimming today, Gwen. I need to go home."

"Is everything okay?" She jumped to her feet. "Are you okay?"

I smiled. "Yeah, I'm good." I felt a little lightheaded though. That was the first time I glimpsed the future. "I'd like you to come to my house tomorrow for lunch or dinner."

She brightened. "Okay. I'd like that too."

"I want GM to meet you."

EIGHTEEN

Gwen's eyes scrunched. "Who's GM?"

I smirked. "That's what I call my grandmother."

"Not Granny? Not Nana?"

I held up a hand like a traffic cop. "Not yet." That was going to change soon, I'm sure. But just not yet. "You'll be able to come though, right?"

"Yeah, sure; it's just down the road, Keira."

"Good. I'll need your phone number before I leave." I turned to head back inside."

"You sure you don't want me to drop you off? It's no big deal."

"No... I need the walk to clear my head." She grasped my arm in a way I had seen Lawrence hold GM. I didn't get any flashes or anything, but I was happy for the support. "I'll just throw my clothes on and head home."

"Okay, Keira." We headed inside together.

***

Coming out of the bathroom after changing, the dog was in

the hallway. He looked up at me and his ears drooped down before he turned, skulking into the bedroom. I sighed and continued on.

Gwen stood next to her father with her hand on his shoulder. She turned from watching the television and smiled. "All set?"

"Yup. Thanks for the beer. We'll get in a swim next time." I moved over to her father. "Nice meeting you, Mr. Jones."

He looked up with a smile. "It's Devon. And don't make yourself scarce, y'hear? My daughter doesn't have enough good friends."

I bent to shake his hand and once more, loneliness emanated into my gut. "I'll be back, don't worry about that. You'll probably get sick of seeing me." I glanced at the framed photo on the table next to him. It showed a young woman in a nurse's uniform holding a bunch of roses. From the set of her wide eyes and cheekbones, it was obviously Gwen's mother. The resemblance was too great for it not to be and the photo was old. Nurses didn't wear those caps anymore.

When I straightened and looked past him a greyish mist was in the corner of the room. My breath caught in my throat. The shape became clearer, a woman in a light dress, staring back at me. It was Gwen's mother. I glanced at Gwen and her dad but they were smiling at me, totally oblivious to the fact that the ghost was there.

Despite what I'd done earlier that day, helping Molly and Sam transition, there was no way I was going to mess with this one. It might not fit into GM's world view, maintaining order and The Veil but it worked for this family.

"Okay. I'm off." I smiled at Gwen, I'll call you about a time for us to get together once I've run it by GM"

She laughed. "GM? How does she like you calling her that?"

"She's fine with it. When you meet her, you'll see. It suits her." I couldn't help grinning as I pictured my grandmother.

"I think I'll stick with Mrs. York, if it's all the same to you." She followed me to the door and stood on the veranda as I walked down the lane.

I turned and my hand rose to mimic a phone call. "I'll talk to you later. Bye!"

I couldn't wait to tell GM all about my visit!

NINETEEN

W ell done, Keira!" GM lifted her glass and then took a long swallow as we sat in the living room before dinner.

I had just finished telling her about seeing the ghost of Gwen's mother, and my impressions when I'd shook hands with Gwen's dad. But I was leaving the best until last. My hands tensed for a moment on the glass I was holding as I looked over at her. "I think I might have found my 'Lawrence'."

She paused, her hand in mid air before setting her glass on the table in front of her. "What?"

I relayed the vision I'd had of the two of us at an airport sometime in the future. I couldn't get the words out fast enough and I popped to my feet, pacing the floor in front of her. "I invited her over so you and Lawrence can meet her! I want to get your impressions. But I'm pretty sure I'm right!"

Lawrence had stepped into the room to let us know about dinner. From the bewildered look on his face, he'd caught enough of the conversation. "The mail lady? This is who you think will act as your *Guardian,* going forward?"

Guardian? He made it sound like being a Guardian was like royalty or something. Plus, this was the first I'd ever heard the term, for what he did. My chin lifted higher as I stared into his eyes. "She's not just a mail lady! I'll have you know that she's a physicist. She was working on her PhD when she had to drop out in order to look after her father. She's incredibly smart, and..." I groped for a word to describe Gwen, but all I could come up with was *"Nice!"* I crossed my arms. "I'm pretty sure we'll make a good team."

"But Keira...there's more to it than being smart. There's loyalty."

"Undying loyalty!" Lawrence tried to underscore GM's words, speaking louder and squaring his shoulders.

GM smiled and looked up at him, the affection showing in her eyes. "Yes. You've proved that more than once, my dear."

His eyebrows bobbed high and he sniffed. "Not to mention, my ability to sense impending danger. I admit, I wasn't born with it but I've trained myself."

"Well... so could she."

GM chimed in, "Not to sound sexist, but the role of guardian would be more appropriate for a man. I mean sometimes, it takes physical strength."

"I'm not worried about that, GM, she's in terrific shape." The discrepancy between Gwen's physical fitness and Lawrence's would be cruel to point out. Especially now that he was starting to warm up to me.

I decided to switch tacks. "All I'm saying is that I want you to meet her. I want to know your impressions. And you can't deny my vision can you? We were together in the future and I know we were about to catch a plane to do *your* work, GM."

She sighed and her gaze flickered over to Lawrence. "Okay. We'll meet Gwen and give you our impressions. I'll keep an open mind." Her eyes turned thoughtful. "But...you need to keep an open mind as well, my girl. Don't just jump at the first person who comes along. Gwen may be nice, physically fit and seem perfect but...she may not *want* the role of Guardian. It's not without peril. And she has her father to look after. She has to know what she's getting in for."

My hands rose before me. "Whoa, whoa, back up. I haven't said that *I* was taking the job. My heart was doing cartwheels in my chest. Gwen would be interested. How could she be a fan of Stephen King and *not be*? "So lunch tomorrow?"

"Not tomorrow. I've got something planned for us that will take up most of the day. How about lunch the day after?" GM looked over the rim of her glass at me as she took a sip.

Lawrence walked over to the sideboard and poured a drink for himself before turning and offering more to us. "She'll be working then, delivering *mail*. The day after tomorrow is Monday, Pamela."

"Don't be a snob, Lawrence." GM held her glass out for a refill.

He topped up her glass and then turned to top me up. "Why don't you ask her for dinner instead? She can come early, have some drinks and I'll prepare something special."

"Of course you must join us, Lawrence. Your input is invaluable." GM batted her eyes at him again. Geeesh! She acted more like a helpless schoolgirl than I did sometimes! I watched Lawrence puff up at her sweet talk and shook my head. "You two..."

Lawrence's eyes darted from GM to me. "What?"

I waved my hands. "Nothing. Forget it. So you really think Gwen coming for dinner's a good idea, Lawrence?"

"I *did* suggest it."

"That's true." I was a little surprised.

He nodded. "Yes. This woman is your candidate, Keira. I think a little more formality would be in order." He cocked his head. "This is important, so let's put our best foot forward."

"Thanks Lawrence. I think she's going to be impressed."

TWENTY

Later that evening, I looked for my cell phone to call Gwen. I slapped myself upside the head when I realized I had left it in her bathroom when I changed. It was a little late, so I figured I'd drop by the next day and pick it up. I'd extend my invitation to dinner for Monday night while I was at it.

***

The next morning was gloomy and it was tempting to just roll over and go back to sleep. Instead, I got up; a half an hour later I joined GM in the sun room.

"Hi, GM" I balanced coffee, a bowl of cereal and a banana tucked between my elbow and waist as I entered.

She had on gardening gloves, a pair of snips in her hand, pruning some dead shoots from a large potted plant. "Good morning, Keira." She turned and a smile twitched her lips. "All quiet in your room now?"

"Too quiet. I never thought I'd say it, but I miss Molly's housekeeping."

GM laughed lightly.

"What's so funny?" I took a bite of my banana as she sat down at the table across from me.

"You are, Keira." She shook her head, her eyebrows elevated in amusement. "A week ago you were a night clubbing, New Yorker. And this morning you're grousing about missing your spectral housekeeper."

I swallowed and chortled myself. "Yeah... how things change, huh? From failed acting student to protector of the Universe in seven days." I glanced around. "So that's it for the free housekeeping though, huh? No more ghostly servants?"

"Well...sort of."

"What do you mean?"

GM made a face. "We still have one more spirit to transition."

"Now wait a second, GM, how long have you been living here?"

"Many years. I moved here when your mother started boarding school."

"And so you let these ghosts stay on all that time?" When she nodded, I asked, "Why?"

"Because they were going to serve a greater purpose by staying than by leaving. I knew I was eventually going to have a successor, and for... well, 'training purposes' I needed them here."

"That's pretty cold. You've kept them prisoner here so you could use them?"

She looked at me sharply. "I beg your pardon! Not at all! Any of them, *all* of them could move on the moment they wanted to. I wasn't holding them against their will at all." She tapped the tabletop. "And furthermore, remember how I tried to explain to you that time is different for them? In their state, they've just been here for a day." She waved her hand around the room. "Time applies to us, not to spirits."

"Still... it rubs me wrong, GM."

She reached over and took my hand. "That's because you're good and kind, Keira. They've been happy to be here, and

Molly and Sam were both happy to leave."

I mulled it over; she had a point, I guess. I shrugged. "Okay, you said there's one more, right?"

"I did, didn't I? Well, this one you won't be too keen on, trust me. But we'll save him till after breakfast."

I paused and swallowed hard. "Oh yeah? Who is this one?" From the look in her eyes, she wasn't looking forward to transitioning this guy.

"I'm not." Damn, she was *good* at that mind reading!

"Why?"

She held my gaze. "Because Jarrod is not a spirit that is pure of heart. Molly was child like in her love, and Sam *was* a child. Jarrod is an adult who committed many crimes before his death."

"He was a bad guy?"

"He did evil things while on this plane, yes."

"So he's afraid of going to hell."

"I don't think there is a hell like they talk about. In fact, I'm not even sure hell exists. What I *do* believe is that Jarrod doesn't want to transition because he believes he's due for punishment on the other side."

"Is he?"

"I really don't know, Keira. What matters is what Jarrod 's soul believes and that fear keeps him here." She paused. "And he doesn't belong here."

"It sounds like we have our work cut out for us then."

"I'm afraid that's not all. A transition like this one has perils."

"Perils. You mean dangers. You mean this can be dangerous."

She closed her eyes and nodded. "Yes," she said softly.

"What kind of dangers?"

"Demonic dangers."

Whoaaaa.

***

A chill went through me. Transitioning Molly and Sam was

hair-raising. Even so, I never had any sense of danger during the event. But now...

"Today, I'm going to teach you about the Ouija board. You need to learn how to use it but I warn you, only do so as a last resort."

"If it's so scary, why use it at all? We did pretty well yesterday with Molly and Sam."

"Good question." GM sat forward and her voice lowered. "Sometimes spirits can be pretty stubborn or just downright weak. The Ouija amps up our ability to communicate with them. The problem is that other entities tune in as well."

"You mean demons? So those movies I've seen pretty much got it right?" My mouth was suddenly dry as dust as I hung onto the edge of my seat. From what I'd seen on screen, there was no way I wanted to see them for real.

She sighed and looked into my eyes. "I'm not going to lie to you...it's frightening sometimes. But that's something else you must learn...how to control your fear." She rose to her feet. "If you're done with your breakfast, we'll move to the living room. When you take your dishes into the kitchen, would you ask Lawrence to join us?"

***

When I walked into the living room, the room was dim. GM had drawn the heavy brocade curtains shut. A single white candle flickered near the end of the coffee table. Next to it was a bundle of dried grass in a large sea shell and a black, pyramid shaped crystal.

GM sat forward in the chair across from the sofa. She had just placed a flat board on the coffee table. My gut tightened when I saw the familiar dark lettering and symbols. The Ouija board. When she placed the leaf shaped pointer on the board's surface, my heart began to hammer in my chest. Oh boy, here we go.

My eyes darted over to Lawrence before I slunk down onto the sofa. I barely dared to breathe as my grandmother's words sounded in my mind—'a last resort'.

"Wait a second, GM," I said. "Before we start, what exactly is the danger we're going to be dealing with here?"

She looked over to Lawrence, and he nodded. Turning back to me, she said, "Did you see the movie 'The Exorcist'?" When I nodded in reply, she said, "That pretty much covers it then."

"Are you kidding me?"

"No, Keira, I'm not. If a demon is strong enough, it can fling things about, using household items like missiles. It can sow confusion in your heart and mind, and it can... if you allow it to—possess you and take over your body and make you do its bidding."

Holy shit this was real.

GM's eyes met mine above the board. "Keira. What is the opposite of love?"

Was this a trick question? Anyone knew the answer to that. "Hate."

"No, it's fear. I can feel your fear and you're right to be cautious. But fear...not only is it crippling, but it can be used as a weapon against you. I have found that facing your fear, instead of denying it, lessens its power. Accept your fear. Then release it with each breath, exhaling it. With every inhalation, you take in love, which is present all around and within you."

I closed my eyes and tried to do what she said.

It didn't work.

"Keira, look at me." I opened them, and watched her eyes. They began to shimmer.

I will not be afraid
Fear is the soul destroyer
And would consume me
Were I allow it
I rebuke fear
To its face of many masks I stare unafraid
One by one, I will watch those masks fall away
Crumble to ash
And drift away
In the breeze of my love
Leaving nothing by myself

And I will still stand
Alone and unafraid.

Her words echoed in my mind and a vision of a pile of ash wafting away from the surface of polished white purity filled my mind's eye.

My mouth hung open. "You did that, GM? You projected your thoughts into my mind?"

"Yes, Keira. I was only able to because of how strong you've become so quickly. I can't do that with anyone, only one gifted as you are." Holding my eyes, she sent that litany to me again. Over and over we repeated it until I was... no longer afraid.

"Now breathe, Keira. Rebuke the fear from you and inhale the love that is this Universe's nature." Together we did the breathing, our inner voices joined with each inhalation and exhalation, over and over.

Now let us begin

"Yes," I said.

Her hands rose and then with just the lightest touch, her fingertips rested on the planchette. Oh God. This was it. My fingers joined hers on the small triangle. There was a tiny tremble in the object that I hoped was the result of one of us, rather than...

"Is there a spirit in the room?" GM's voice almost made me jump out of my skin and my gaze darted around the room.

The planchette vibrated and then jerked to the right! It stopped on the word 'Yes'. My fingers tingled, like there was a small current of electricity running from the small object to my hands.

"What is your name?" GM's voice was soft yet there was a commanding authority to it as well.

The planchette slid across the board to the letter 'J' and then to 'A' and 'R'.

It then slid to the center of the board. It began to vibrate under our fingers. I stared at it, then looked up to GM. She watched the planchette intently, so I dropped my eyes back down.

The object darted to the 'L'. I tried swallowing in a mouth that was dry as dust all of a sudden.

The planchette moved quickly through the other letters pausing only a beat on each one. 'E', 'A','V', 'E.'

My eyes met my grandmothers and hers became narrower with purpose.

"What is your name?" When there was no reply, she repeated herself, louder and more commanding. "GIVE US YOUR NAME!" The power in her voice startled me.

The candle flame flickered, then blazed up, casting long shadows to the corners of the room. The air became colder and...dense. It became harder to breathe, and a stench suddenly filled the room. My heart pounded faster. There was something here in the room with us! It was totally unlike what I'd experienced with Molly or Sam. Whatever this was...it didn't like us one little bit. *I will not be afraid*...I thought to myself.

Once more the planchette jerked, moving so fast through the same series of letters that it was hard to keep my fingers attached to it. L E A V E

GM's nostrils flared as she took a deep breath. "Jarrod Blythe. Are you here with us?"

My eyes were marbles watching GM. She knew the name of the ghost, why did she have to ask its name?

The small object began to circle under the arc of letters, vibrating again. It started to drift towards the word 'YES' printed on the board but was yanked back to its circling pattern. I could sense a struggle happening right under my fingers.

"Why do you not answer me, Jarrod?" GM's gaze was like a laser beam on the planchette.

The movement was slow and tremulous. 'A', 'F', 'R', 'A', 'T'—

The small object shot to the word on the bottom part of the board. 'GOODBYE'. Then it flew out from under our fingers across the room, bouncing against a bookcase.

We were cast into darkness when the candle flickered and

died. I sensed movement to my right and Lawrence stepped by me. He picked up the candle and lit it again. "Pamela. You need to end this." He picked up the bundle of grass and flicked the lighter, setting fire to the ends of it.

The acrid smell of the smoke drifted from where he held the smouldering herb. "Jarrod's spirit was not alone, you know that. It's time to cleanse the room."

GM sighed and nodded, sitting back in her seat. I didn't have to be asked twice to do the same. I took a deep breath and waited for her to speak. All the while, Lawrence wandered around the room, holding the smudge before him like a torch. I didn't want to say anything about the fact that the smoke smelled like weed, although knowing Lawrence marijuana would be the last thing he'd ever have.

"And this, my dear, is why I dislike the Ouija board. Jarrod was here and would have communicated with us if not for that *'thing'* that managed to butt in." Her hand rose to stroke her neck and she stared above, deep in thought for a moment.

"It was... a demon?"

"Some kind of demon, yes. When they refuse to give you their name, it's a dead giveaway." Her eyes rolled and she beat me to the punch. "No pun intended."

"So what do we do now? Give up on this Jarrod guy?"

She nodded. "For the time being. I'll keep trying to coax him from the shadows but as far as this bloody board goes, we'll wait until the energy in this house has been rejuvenated." She gazed over at Lawrence who was still waving the smudge through the air, walking around the room. "That's what Lawrence is doing now, Keira. The sage smudge is something I picked up from Native lore. It helps to cleanse the atmosphere of negative energy."

Lawrence pulled the drapes open, letting in more light from the gray day outside. Even so, the room seemed glum and heavy.

"Can we go back to the sunroom now?" There were things I wanted to know about these demons but asking them in here didn't appeal to me.

"One moment, Keira." Lawrence walked over and held the smudge high. "Stand up and let this cleanse you."

I got to my feet and stepped closer to him. His hand gently fluttered the bundle of smoldering embers. Like incense, the grey mist floated over my body and face. He ended at my toes and then turned to GM. For a moment, I wished it *was* marijuana. Getting a buzz would take the edge off for sure.

When Lawrence was done with GM, we headed back into the sunroom. Just entering the room made it easier to breathe. I could see why it was her favourite spot in the house. We both sat at the small table where we usually sat together, and Lawrence leaned against the entranceway.

I had to ask. "Where are these demons from, GM? You say that you don't know if there's a hell, so where did they come from?"

"I'm not sure, but I've come to believe that they are beings that battle the forces of Nature."

"Forces of Nature?"

She nodded. "Yes. Nature is Order, Harmony and Love. And the greatest of these is Love. These beasts are Chaos, Conflict and Fear. Their greatest weapon is Fear. They're the ones of the spirit realm who wish to weaken The Veil because they crave Chaos." She held up her finger to make a point. "They feed on *fear*, Keira. That's why it's important to go beyond your fear. You have to remember that you are at one with the Universe; all that is good. That will be the source of your strength."

I nodded. "I will, GM."

She looked past me to where Lawrence was standing at the passageway into the sunroom. They silently stared for a moment, and nodded in unison. Turning back to me, she took a deep breath. "How did you feel when we used the Ouija board? Think about your answer for a minute."

I sat back and looked down at my lap for a little while. "It was frightening, even with the litany."

"It would have been much more so without the litany. It's a litany, Keira; not a magic spell. Go on."

"I sensed the air change when that thing, whatever it was, started shoving that planchette around. I could feel a rage. It really didn't want us trying to help Jarrod." I blinked rapidly. "He's a prisoner to that thing."

She nodded. "Yes. It's going to be a battle to help that poor soul. He was a weak man when he lived and he never changed."

"Who was he? What do you know about him?"

"I managed to do some research. Back in the 1920's he was a crafty weasel. He was a bootlegger, but he was also an informer to the police. He played both sides against each other for his own profit."

"Oh. A Wall Street broker, you mean?"

She flashed a quick smile. "Well, he was as much a scoundrel as they are, there's no doubt of that. But he and his colleagues were murderous thugs, Keira. He took part in several killings; then framed an innocent man who was hanged."

"And you want to *help* him?"

She was silent for a moment. "I want to protect The Veil," she finally said. "Look, dear—we're all sinners to one degree or another. We're also saints. Yes, Jerrod did those things. But he also looked after people he didn't have to. He provided for several families who lost husbands—fathers— in the Great War."

"Oh."

"I'm not," and she pointed at me, "nor are you, in position to be a judge of this man's soul. I have a calling to protect The Veil."

"I understand GM; this is bigger than Jarrod."

The picture of a weasely, thinly built man, his beard rough and unkempt, with long stringy hair flashed in my mind. I gazed at GM and she nodded. That was the guy we were trying to help?

"Everyone needs help, Keira. Even Jarrod. But it's The Veil we must defend."

TWENTY ONE

Five minutes later, I pulled into Gwen's driveway, parking behind her truck. The rain had really picked up; by the time I got to her front porch I was soaked. I knocked on the door and waited.

Nobody answered, so I knocked again, louder. After the third time, her dad pulled it open.

"Keira! What a pleasant surprise." Leaning on his walker, he stepped aside and bade me to come in. As he closed the door, he looked down the hallway and back at me, his smile faltering.

"Were you at the door long?" he asked.

"Yeah, I had to knock three times. It's no big deal, I mean with the storm—"

He cut me off. "A couple of minutes ago, Buster jumped up, started whining like crazy and took off out the back door of the house." Devon stared at me like I was a specimen. "I don't know how he managed to do it, but he opened the latch on the screen door with his snout and took off out the back yard. He's standing against the back fence and won't come in. I came back in to get Gwen when I heard you knocking." He looked back again towards the rear of the house, let out a small sigh and turned back to me. "He's never done that before; he always knew when someone pulled into the driveway and would start barking at the front door." He held my eyes.

"Yeah... that is weird, isn't it?" I said weakly.

"Buster's afraid of you."

I bit my lower lip. "I know," I mumbled.

"I mean, really afraid of you."

I looked down at the floor. "Yeah." I raised my eyes. "Dogs never liked me, but lately it's gotten worse." I shrugged. "Maybe I should use a different shampoo or something?" I tried to smile at my totally lame excuse and failed.

Devon looked towards the back of the house again. "Well, he'll come in when he's ready, I guess," he said. "He'll be soaking wet, but it's not cold out and that's where he wants to be... for now." He turned back to me. "You left your phone in the bathroom."

"Thanks. Can I talk to Gwen?"

His head turned and he yelled. "HEY GWEN! KEIRA'S HERE FOR HER PHONE!"

Grinning, she came downstairs, holding my cell phone. "I was going to drive over to your place with this when the rain stopped."

I shoved it into my pocket. "Instead of coming for lunch, how would you like to come for dinner tomorrow night? GM and Lawrence asked if you'd join us for dinner."

She looked over at her father. His hand arced in the air and he turned. "Don't worry about me. I'll throw a pizza in the oven and catch the Jays game."

Gwen turned back to me. "What time? I'd love to! Dinner beats lunch, any old day." She tilted her head towards the kitchen. "Want a beer?"

There was a guilty feeling in the pit of my stomach. She didn't know she was interviewing for Lawrence's job. How much could I actually tell her? "Just a Coke." I hung my jacket up and toed my sneakers before following her to the kitchen.

As I passed by the living room, where Gwen's dad was now getting settled in his usual chair, I glanced in the corner where I'd seen her mother the day before. But there was no sign of her.

I took a seat at the table and waited for Gwen to finish pouring a large bottle of coke into two glasses. "So... am I going to meet those ghosts? Molly and Sam?"

She got right to it. "No... they're gone."

She made a small frown. "That's pretty convenient. You tell me about ghosts in that place, and just before I come over, they've 'gone'."

I snorted, thinking of the episode with Jerrod. Convenient wasn't the word I was thinking of. "Sorry to disappoint you." I pointed my chin at her. "What would you ever do if you actually saw one?"

She leaned forward and her eyes became wide. "Are you *kidding* me? That would be the most awesome thing." Her smile faded. "I wish sometimes, I could see my mother."

It was the perfect opening for me. My voice lowered, despite the din of the T.V. in the background. "What would you say if I told you I saw your mother here yesterday?" I watched her closely. But her eyes weren't shocked, just a little sad.

She was silent for a few beats before she spoke, "If it wasn't for what happened yesterday beside the pool when you read my mind or something, I wouldn't believe you...but, I do. I've felt her presence but I've never actually seen her. I envy you that ability."

I blew softly from puffed out cheeks, my eyes on the glass in front of me. "It's only happened since I've been with my grandmother. She's a sensitive about these things and it seems I've inherited it. And her house...if anything supernatural was going to happen, believe me that house would bring it out." I took a sip of the pop. "You said so yourself, that house has mystical properties."

She nodded and sat down opposite me. "Yeah, it does. I don't know about your grandmother, but that rose blooming in the dead of winter is something off the wall, that's for sure." The flecks of her eyes were green in spots, rimmed by long dark eyelashes, devoid of any make-up. With the smattering of freckles across the bridge of her nose, she was the poster child for the girl next door.

I shook my head. "Ghosts in a bedroom? Flowers blooming in January? That doesn't freak you out?" If anyone had told me this a few weeks ago, I would have been freaked out. Now, it was just another day at GM's curiosity house.

She slapped the table lightly with her hand. "Are you kidding me? That would be fascinating!"

"More fascinated than scared? This stuff scares people, Gwen."

"Not me." She chuckled. "Maybe I'm too stupid to be scared."

"Yeah, right. I think too curious."

She eyed me. "I think there's something going on with you and your grandmother and I'd like to find out more."

I smiled, sipping my drink. That was one hurdle crossed. The interest and lack of fear was one thing but...what about her father? If I did take this up, and take over for GM, would Gwen be free to come with me?

God! Look at me! I was already planning a career with this!

More and more, my thoughts were turning to accepting the mantle from GM. Had I already made up my mind?

TWENTY TWO

I was waiting for Gwen in the parlour when the doorbell rang. I didn't want to take the chance that Lawrence would greet her stiffly, so I called to the back of the house "I got it!" before he could appear.

I swung the heavy oak door open and my jaw dropped.

Gwen stood there in heels and make-up. Her 'Girl Next Door' natural look was elevated to a downright charming level. Even her hair was loose, the dark mane flowing over the shoulders of a light lime green linen dress that ended a couple inches above her knee.

She noticed my eyes boggling and did a quick twirl. "I hope I didn't overdo it. You did say that your grandmother likes to gussy up for dinner."

"You nailed it, don't worry." Even so, I felt a little shabby in my jean skirt and top.

Stepping into the entrance hall, she gave her head a small shake. "I can't remember the last time I got dressed up to go to someone's house for dinner." She looked over to me. "Dates at restaurants? Sure. Weddings and such? Absolutely. But

156

doing this to visit with my neighbours? That's a new one."

I nodded as I shut the door behind her. "It's been 'dressing for dinner' every night since I arrived." I glanced back towards where the living room was. "And I'll bet GM has been doing it all along. Pretty Old School, huh?"

She made a small shrug. "I don't know... I think it's kind of elegant. Making a thing out of sharing a meal every night... it's kind of cool, don't you think?"

I scoffed. "You do it every night, and we'll see."

She laughed lightly. "You might have a point, but I'd sure love to find out."

"I don't know, Gwen; I think those 'genteel times' are kind of gone with the wind."

Before she could reply, Lawrence appeared from the living room archway. "Gwen, isn't it? It's nice to meet you instead of just seeing you on your route." He took her hand and even did a slight bow as he smiled at her. "I'm Lawrence Brady, Mrs. York's assistant."

"How do you do," she replied. "It's nice of you and Mrs. York to invite me. I've always admired this house and wondered what it would be like inside. I never imagined that I'd be invited here for dinner."

His hand extended pointing the way to the living room. "This way, please. Mrs. York is in the living room."

I led the way to where GM was seated on the large sofa. We crossed over to her and I made introductions.

"Thank you for asking me to dinner, Mrs. York. I've been looking forward to it all day."

Taking in Gwen's outfit, GM smiled and nodded. "It's nice to meet Keira's friend, even though we've obviously seen you around. Would you care for a drink? Lawrence makes a mean gimlet."

Gwen looked nervous as she answered, "Do you have beer? I'm afraid I'm not much of a liquor fan. I developed a taste for beer in university and now that's all I drink."

At GM's sharp jerk of her head backwards, Gwen spoke again, her words tumbling all over themselves. "I mean, that's not all I drink. I drink water and pop and well—"

GM laughed lightly. "I know what you meant, dear." She turned to Lawrence. "We have beer in the fridge, don't we?"

"Yes, of course." He walked out of the room.

GM patted the seat on the sofa beside her. "Please sit down, Gwen," She held her glass out to me. "Would you mind topping me up, dear?" As I poured a drink for myself and GM, she continued, "Keira tells me you studied to be a physicist?"

"Yes. I was doing graduate work when my dad became ill. To be honest, I actually like what I'm doing now. My evenings and weekends are my own, with no papers to write or any lab work. I mean, aside from taking care of Dad."

"Your father is ill?"

Handing GM her fresh drink, I sat in the armchair beside them. I was positive GM knew everything about Gwen's dad, and watched the interplay between them.

Gwen nodded. "Yes. He's had M.S. for years, but when my mother passed away three years ago he had a terrible episode. He was hospitalized for a month. When he was released, I had already suspended my studies and had gotten on full time with the Post Office."

"Oh my poor dear." GM reached out and stroked Gwen's shoulder. She turned to me and arched an eyebrow. "How sad, Keira," she said aloud. *'This could be a problem for you dear'* echoed in my head.

"He didn't seem too ill when I saw him," I said.

"I know," said Gwen. "The attacks—they call them 'relapses'—come out of nowhere. Sometimes he just gets worn down, but he's collapsed a couple of times."

Lawrence came in and passed her a pilsner glass filled with beer. She took it and took a deep sip while he took a seat.

"That must be hard on you, dear. When I was your age, I liked to travel...see the world. But I suppose, for you..." GM's voice trailed off but she watched Gwen closely.

Gwen sat primly on the sofa, her long legs folded together to the side. "Oh, I manage to get away every now and then. Just last year I went to the States on a sightseeing tour of Civil

War mansions. My brother Sean stays with Dad."

I glanced at Lawrence and GM. Gwen wasn't as tied to her routine as they'd thought. "Old houses? You would pass up the beach to see a bunch of old houses?"

Gwen snorted. "Seen one beach, you've seen 'em all as far as I'm concerned." She looked around the living room. "Older homes have... character." She looked to GM and continued. "Like this house. It's almost as big as some of the plantation homes I visited you know. I'll bet there are stories that these walls could tell us if they could speak."

The two of them gazed at each other silently for a moment. Finally, GM smiled sweetly. "What sort of stories do you suppose, dear?"

Gwen glanced over to me and back at GM before speaking. "Well, for one thing, did you know its history when you bought it Mrs. York?" Without waiting for an answer she continued, "Did you know it once harboured a rum runner? The guy's body was found in the cellar. The police never knew if his death was suicide or if he was murdered."

GM's smile dropped like a stone when she looked across at Gwen. "I've come to know of that. You are a student of local history, then? I know the house has a reputation for being a bit...odd."

"This house is haunted isn't it, Mrs. York?"

I saw Lawrence stiffen. GM didn't bat an eye. "What an interesting question."

"You didn't answer it, ma'am." Whoaaa... Gwen wasn't backing off a whit.

"No, I didn't." GM smiled sweetly again. "The answer is yes."

***

Her reply hung in the air for a moment.

Gwen tilted her head and nodded slightly. "Thank you, Mrs. York. I appreciate your honesty." She looked over to me and back at GM. "Keira tells me it's not as haunted as it had been."

GM nodded. "Yes, that's true. Molly and Sam have moved on." She leaned her head in to Gwen slightly. "The ironic part is that the man you just described who died here *is* still about."

"Really?" Gwen's eyes lit up and she looked around the room. "Right now? He's here? Can you see him?" She put her hand on GMs forearm. *"Could I see him?"*

GM's mouth turned downward. "No, dear, he's not present at this time."

"How do you get him to show up? Could we use one of those Ouija boards or something to get him to show up?"

GM's eyes flashed. "Absolutely not! That is a dangerous instrument!"

"Whoa… take it easy, GM, she's just asking a question," I said.

GM huffed a sigh. "Excuse me for my outburst, Gwen." She pursed her lips for a moment. "As far as the spirit that's still here, and encountering him…even if he was here right now, you wouldn't be able to see him anyway." She gestured towards me. "Myself and my granddaughter have that gift, yes; but—"

Lawrence cut her off. "But it's a rare gift, Gwen. I've never seen any of the spirits in all the years I've been with Mrs. York." He gave a mild laugh. "I've seen their handiwork, but I've never seen them."

"Handiwork?"

He nodded. "If they get upset, they are able to move things."

"Like in the movies? Things flying around? Stuff like that?"

"Yes. And the chill in the room…"

"Don't forget the smells, Lawrence," GM piped in. She grimaced. "Sometimes they've been known to have disgusting smells."

Eyes wide, Gwen stared at each of us in turn. "You're telling me the truth."

"Afraid so," I said.

"And yet," GM added, "this doesn't seem to frighten you. Why is that?" She looked at Gwen with frank curiosity.

"Because I find it fascinating. Did you know in Physics, there's a branch of it that is trying to figure out the relationship between consciousness and matter?" She held up her hand. "Now these researchers are kind of out there, but they're asking some hard science questions about the nature of the mind, the body…" her voice faded.

"And the soul," I said.

Gwen nodded, pensively. "And the soul, yes." She looked up at me. "You've *seen* my mother's soul at my house, right?" When I nodded in reply, her eyes filmed with tears. "Can you communicate with her? Can you say something to her for me?"

"I don't know, to be honest." I said. I looked over to GM; this wasn't anything we've talked about. "Can we, GM?"

"Communicate with the dead? Be a medium between the dead and the living?" She shook her head. "No. That's not what we're supposed to do, Keira." She looked to Gwen. "I'm sorry, my dear, but I'm unable to be a messenger between those who have died and those of us still on this level of existence."

"Why?" she asked, her voice rising. "It would give such comfort to those of us left behind!"

"My work is of a different nature."

"And what is your work?"

GM sighed. "We'll discuss that another time, dear."

Before Gwen could push the issue, Lawrence stepped forward. "Gwen, I'd love to give you a tour of this house. Would you care to join me?"

Gwen's lips became a thin line. "I'll hold you to that, Mrs. York. I'd love to know just what your 'work' is." She stood.

Lawrence held out the crook of his arm and she took it. "Let's start with the top floor," he said. "I'll tell you the stories of Molly and Sam." They left the room and headed for the hallway.

I turned to GM. "Well, what do you think?"

"Her concern for her father will be an issue, Keira. And what will she think when she learns of just what your duties are?"

"What's that supposed to mean? You protect The Veil, and that's what you want me to do. So what?"

She shook her head in disappointment. "And just how do we maintain the integrity of The Veil?"

"By helping spirits move on." I stopped and it hit me. "Oh shit."

"Indeed."

I looked towards the staircase where Gwen and Laurence had ascended and lowered my voice. "Spirits like Gwen's mother."

GM nodded. "And how do you think she would feel about that? Losing her mother all over again?"

Damn, she was right. I sat up straight in my chair. "Hey, I didn't say I was taking the job, GM, I was just thinking if you thought she would be a good replacement for Lawrence, *should* I take the job."

She leaned over to me. "You're going to have to make that decision quite soon, dear. As far as Gwen is concerned, I'd rather hear Lawrence's opinion before rendering my own judgement.

I sat back in my chair. Why did she say that I'd have to make up my mind soon?

***

After her tour of the house, the four of us all agreed that further discussions of the supernatural could wait for another time.

That's not to say that the dinner wasn't a smashing success. We had a wonderful evening together; the conversation sparkled. We discussed religion and politics roundly; it got pretty lively at times, especially when Gwen went on a tangent about Wall Street investors. But the cool thing was that each time it started getting heated, Lawrence (who woulda thunk?) defused the situation with a witty bon mot that made the rest of us start laughing.

After dessert and coffee, Gwen stood, thanked us for a wonderful evening, and got ready to leave. I saw her out.

In the foyer, I put my hand on her arm. "I hope you can keep this all confidential, Gwen."

She looked at me with wide eyed innocence. "What? That your grandmother loves vodka gimlets in the evening?"

"Very funny."

"Well... I am sorely tempted to contact the National Enquirer with this story, for sure. A grandmother/granddaughter tag team of ghost hunters living with their Old Man Friday in a hundred and forty year old mansion." She tilted her head at me. "Think they'd pay me for the tip?"

My face fell. "You're kidding. Right?"

She slapped my back. "Of course, silly. I'd be the one who would look looney tunes." She looked over my shoulder towards the living room. "What I don't understand is just what the old gal does with that gift you two share." She turned back to me. "I mean, you could help a lot of grieving people by communicating with them you know."

I crossed my arms. "People like you, you mean." Boy was I stupid telling her I saw her mother's spirit.

"Yeah, people like me!" Her eyes filmed again. "Just to be able to..."

"Tell her you love her? That you and your dad miss her?"

"Yes!"

I reached out for her. "Gwen... *she knows that*. And from the look on her face, she loves and misses you guys too."

"It's not fair. I'm her flesh and blood, and I can't see her, but you can." She looked at the open door. "I'm heading home. Why don't you stop by tomorrow?"

"Okay. Maybe we'll get an actual swim in, huh?" I knew she was planning on working on me more about communicating with her mother. And to be honest, I didn't have a problem with it. When I put my hand on her, the black and bleak sorrow in her was almost overwhelming. I wasn't going to stand idly by if there was anything I could do to ease such pain. No matter what GM would think of that.

We said our goodbyes and I closed the door behind her.

I raced into the living room where Lawrence and GM were sharing a night cap. How did they do it? After downing a bottle of wine with dinner, cocktails before and still they were fine with a glass of brandy?

I took a seat across from them on the sofa. "Well?" My gaze was firmly on Lawrence.

He glanced at G.M and then smiled looking at me. "Gwen is a lovely girl. She's smart. She's able to study hard, so she has the discipline to learn."

My fingers fisted my hair at each side of my head. There it was...the interminable 'but'. "Okay, I surrender; what's the problem?"

"I don't think she'll abandon her responsibilities to her father. You and she are friends but the emotional tie isn't there." He dropped his head. "I genuinely like her, Keira, but I'm unable to see how it could work."

GM reached over and patted his hand. "I trust your judgement in this, dear. You may not have my abilities to the extent that I do, but still, you know the role and what it entails. If you have doubts..." She turned to look sadly at me. "...then it's probably best to move on right now. Maybe you'll be on your own like I was for a few years before I met Lawrence."

My stomach dropped to the floor. For a moment I sat there silently, wondering at the depth of disappointment I was feeling. In one respect, they were right. I didn't know Gwen very well at all...but then why was I feeling this sense of loss?

It made no sense at all, and I went to bed with a heavy heart.

TWENTY THREE

I opened my eyes the next morning feeling… well, sad. I know it's stupid—I had only met Gwen a few days ago, and last night was only the fifth time we were together. But there it was. If that vision I had by her pool of us in the future at an airport was wrong, then how could I trust any of my so called gifts? On the other hand, her ties to her father… how could I presume to come between them? So yeah, when I headed down for breakfast I was sad and confused.

Seeing my expression as I entered the sun room, GM tried to be consoling. "Keira. You will meet the right person to help you."

"Easy for you to say, GM" I said as I took my usual seat. "You've had Lawrence by your side for years and years."

"Yes, but I did go through a period where I was on my own." She looked sharply back at me. "What I'm trying to tell you is to be strong in and of yourself. You have a gift, and you have an important role to fulfill. So get over it and move on, young lady."

Oh man, she went from consoling to insistent in a

heartbeat. "Thanks for all the sympathy."

She huffed. "You want sympathy? For not upsetting your friend's life? A friend you hardly know?"

"There's a connection between us." I could feel my back getting up.

She snorted. "I disagree. You expect this woman to abandon her father to help you with your work?"

"Gwen wouldn't be abandoning him! We could hire someone to look after him! What's the big deal?"

"Keira, I don't want you rushing into something and making a mistake. In the long run it can cost you dearly."

I huffed out a breath. "Oh yeah? Once again, that's pretty easy for you to say."

That really got to her. She sat up straight, blue fire in her eyes. "You silly girl. When it comes to rushing into something with the wrong person, I certainly know what those costs can be."

"Yeah, sure."

She rapped the tip of her cane on the floor. "Let me tell you, being an unwed mother in the late 1960's was no picnic, Keira." Her lips made a thin line. "No matter how much wealth one had, one was always… judged. I was under considerable pressure when I learned I was pregnant." Her mouth turned downward. "My doctor advocated giving the baby up for adoption." She sighed. "But worse than that, Susan's father wanted me to have an abortion." She stared at her teacup, turning it on the saucer. "That was the last straw between us."

I pushed my half eaten plate of fruit and yogurt away. "Which brings up my grandfather. You told me you had no idea who he is! I found that hard to believe when you told me that. At least you're being *honest* now!" If she was going to be so insistent with regards to Gwen, I was going to get a little of my own back at her.

"I had my reasons for being…misleading. I can tell you, the man who is your grandfather isn't a man you would like to know. At one time I thought he was dashing, handsome. I didn't want to acknowledge his darker side."

My mouth fell open as she spoke. So she knew who it was. I was right! A picture of a dark haired, athletic man in tennis shorts and a light shirt flashed in my mind. He was classically handsome, with dark eyes and a strong jaw. I couldn't help but grin. It was obvious that she hadn't meant to send that image to me. I'd picked it up all on my own! "GM! He was hot!"

I stifled the chuckle that threatened to burst forth at the indignation in her eyes at me being able to grasp that image from her mind. I decided to press on about her past. "Why did you get pregnant then? Were you two guys married?"

She shook her head. "No. We were living a carefree life and I was on the pill." She raised her eyes to mine. "Which works 99% of the time. One time out of a hundred, it doesn't." She made a wistful smile. "Which is why your mother's middle name is Oona; it was the closest I could come to 'One'."

I had completely forgotten about Gwen at that point; I was excited to learn about family history that had been hidden from me for so long. "So what happened? How did you guys meet?"

She made a rueful smile. "It was the 'Summer of Love' in 1967, and I was in San Francisco." She shook her head wistfully again. "The positive energy in that place for that summer was incredible, Keira. I was drawn to it like a moth to a flame. My gifts were still merely budding."

"No ghost nudging yet?"

"That's right. That came later. Back then, I was able to earn my living gambling. I could pick horse races, or sporting event outcomes with astonishing accuracy. And it was through those endeavours I met David Holmes. Back then, gambling outside of Las Vegas was pretty much the purview of criminals, and David ran an establishment for the local mob in my area."

"Ooohh.. a 'bad boy'."

She nodded. "He seduced me to try to learn my 'secrets'." She shrugged. "To be honest with you, we probably seduced each other." Her eyes glittered. "It was torrid, let me tell you. We were both passionate—"

"You mean horny."

"Don't be crude. We were both passionately in love, and very strong willed." She paused and stared at the floor. "Being with him, though… caused my gift to develop dramatically." She looked back up to me. "And… in some way I still don't understand, it instilled a form of that gift within him too."

"What do you mean?"

"He started to develop powerful 'hunches' about people."

"He could read minds too?"

"Not to the degree you and I are able to, no. But he could tell people's desires… and their weaknesses." She held up a finger. "And that extra… edge, or whatever it was… he used to advance himself up the ranks of his Organization."

"He became a mob boss? Like a Godfather type?"

"He became ruthless, yes. But he always stayed behind the scenes." She shook her head. "That sort of life was repugnant to me, and so I left him. I changed my name and disappeared."

"He never tried to find you or his daughter? That's cold."

GM smiled. "When a person with my abilities decide they don't wish to be found, they're not found, Keira."

"So where is he now?"

"I'm not sure. I've hesitated to keep tabs on him in order to keep your mother—and you—safe from him."

"What do you mean?"

"Before I left him, he was becoming more and more evil, Keira. He had a taste of the power from the beyond and found it intoxicating. He wanted that power for his own ends, not for a greater good. I use my gifts to bring peace to lost souls. He uses what he has to further his own ends. The further you keep yourself from him, the better, Keira." She blinked and her eyes closed for a few moments. "Promise me, you will never try to contact him." Her eyes became misty as she gazed at me. "It's for you…your safety that I ask this. Promise me."

My shoulders fell lower and I exhaled slowly. This was really important to her, if she was on the verge of tears. "I promise."

She straightened and her chin rose, pushing up from the chair. "Good. Now if you're ready, I think we should have another go at contacting Jarrod. He's waited long enough to leave this sphere, don't you think?"

I sighed. Back to the ghost grind, Keira.

TWENTY FOUR

For a moment, I paused before getting to my feet to join her. She'd just dumped a load of information on me and now was brushing it off like the lint she was perpetually finding with her thin fingers. It would take some serious will power to not do a Google search for my grandfather...but I'd give it a try for her sake.

I took a deep breath, shaking the image of my grandfather from my brain. It was immediately replaced by another disturbing thought. "We aren't going to use the Ouija board again, are we?" I asked.

"Most likely."

"Why? It didn't help the last time."

She tugged the collar of her shirt higher. "I know that, Keira. But we won't have a choice. It increases our ability to reach those spirits who don't want to be reached."

"And *others*." I stood up. "Like *demons*."

"I know. It's a risk we must take. For Jerrod's sake, and for the sake of The Veil. His presence here is weakening it, Keira. If we transition him, my hope is that the demon that's attached itself to him will be banished."

"Oh, alright then." The thought popped into my head. "Wait a minute. Is that what happened before?"

Her face took on a sheepish look. "Ummm... I don't know. I've never encountered a demon so strong before. We'll hope for the best, shall we?" With that she turned to the living room.

Oh boy. "Buckle up, Keira," I said aloud. "It's going to be a bumpy ride." My knees were only shaking a little bit as I followed her out to the living room.

Lawrence was already in there. He had the drapes all pulled closed and was going around the room with the smouldering bundle of sage again. "Hey, Lawrence," I said, "don't you do that at the end of the session?"

"I'm hedging our bets, Keira. I don't like this any more than you do." He gazed at GM as she hobbled over to her seat on the couch. "But Pamela has decided, and my job is to support her."

GM's face was resolute, but she nodded in appreciation to him as she took her seat.

I nodded. "If it's any consolation, I'm not looking forward to it either. What is with this spirit that we have to use that thing?" I knew GM didn't like using it, so why bother? What was so important about this guy that she and I couldn't just call him ourselves? Convince him to leave?

GM was staring silently straight ahead, so Lawrence answered. "For one thing, he's very frightened."

"He's not the only one." I muttered under my breath. I had no wish for some demon to hitchhike a ride with Jarrod and the Ouija board was definitely the way for that to happen.

"Yes, but you're strong. And getting stronger by the minute. Now, let me complete the cleansing ritual." He nodded over to a shelf. "If you would set up the candle and the pyramid crystal on the table I'd appreciate it."

I did as I was asked, and took my place opposite GM as Lawrence waved the bundle of smoking sage over each of us. My hand reached into the pocket of my slacks and gripped the tourmaline stone GM had given me a few days ago. It felt smooth in my hand. I hoped all this mumbo jumbo with sage and stones was going to help. I closed my eyes and began to do the breathing exercises she taught me. I opened them, and GM nodded.

"Let us begin," she said.

We both leaned forward, our fingers lightly touching the planchette, while Lawrence took his place in a chair by the door.

"Jarrod Blythe, I ask that you come forward. Are you here with us?" GM spoke like she was a teacher calling out to an unruly kid.

The planchette began to vibrate, slowly at first and then faster and faster. My breath caught in my throat. It started moving slowly to the side of the board where the word 'yes' was written, but stopped just shy of it.

GM huffed a fast sigh and spoke again. "Jarrod, you must leave this plane." Immediately the planchette shot to the word 'no', circling it in small, jerky movements.

"Are you afraid to go?" GM glanced over at me and her chin rose higher.

I sat on the edge of my seat, barely able to keep contact with the small triangle when it swooped across the board to the word 'Goodbye'. It was so much like the last time, the abrupt ending. But GM wasn't having any of it this time.

She took a deep breath and continued; the determination showing in her tight lips. "We aren't through here, Jarrod. I know that you are frightened, but you don't belong here anymore. Will you take the next step and leave this plane of existence?"

Once more the planchette skimmed over the board, stopping at the letters: 'C A N N O T D O O M. '

Cannot doom? He couldn't leave and was doomed? Clearly, not every spirit could be persuaded to leave. Some were beyond helping, even for someone like my grandmother.

Again, the image of a thin, weasel type guy cowering in a corner, flashed in my mind. It was pointless to try to reason with him. He was a terrified little man. Without warning, his image swirled, dissolving into a cloud of black and purple vapour.

Suddenly the planchette began moving once more.

'K I E R' My heart was in my mouth when the next letter it stopped at was an 'A'.

GM gasped. "What about Keira?"

But the small gadget wasn't through yet. It continued on: 'G W E N'.

My grandmother jerked back, almost relinquishing her touch on the planchette.

"What does that mean? Why my name and then Gwen's?" I edged forward, my eyes darting from GM to the board. But the answer wasn't in my grandmother's eyes. She looked as spooked by this as I felt. My heart pounded against my ribs so hard I thought it would jump out.

The breath caught in my throat when the planchette shot to the 'Goodbye'. I jerked my hands back and stared at GM Lawrence was already on his feet striding towards us.

"What did that mean? Why did it say my name and Gwen's?" My fingers trembled as I pulled the tourmaline stone from my pocket and held it in my lap. This was supposed to be a communication with Jarrod and I hadn't said a word but I was being singled out? And not just me, but Gwen?

GM looked down at the floor, and her forehead was lined with deep furrows. "I don't know."

Lawrence picked up the bundle of sage again and fished a lighter from his pocket. He flicked the lighter and brought the flame up to the charred end.

Without warning, we were completely enveloped in a black and purple cloud. It spun around us with a whooshing noise. I could barely see GM through the haze, and the stench of it made my breakfast roll in my stomach. GM's face showed she was as shocked as I.

I looked over to where Lawrence was. He was as still as a statue; frozen in place. In spite of the rushing noise from the disgusting mist, the flame was completely still. I tried to speak, but my throat was frozen.

"Enough!" GM's scream was so loud, her voice cracked.

The cloud condensed into a long, writhing tube. It circled the room once more before evaporating through the wall.

"What just happened?" Lawrence asked. I turned back to him. He was holding the flame to the smudging bundle. "Something just happened, didn't it?"

"Did you see that?" I said.

"See what? I thought I heard Pamela say something." He lifted his eyes from the sage to GM and gasped. "Pamela!" He dropped the sage.

I leapt from my seat. GM was laying back against the seat cushions gasping. Her hair was completely dishevelled and her hand was on her heaving chest. "I…" she gulped for air, "I need to go to my room now."

Lawrence elbowed me out of the way, and lifted her into his arms. I followed.

"I'll call an ambulance!"

"Absolutely not!" they both said in unison. I stopped dead in my tracks.

Lawrence turned to me. "No, Keira; your grandmother is having a spell is all. There's medicine in her room, and she'll be alright shortly. She just needs to lie down and collect herself."

"Lawrence! She looks like she's having a stroke!" I strode up to him in a rage.

GM lifted her head. "No, dear; listen to me." Her breath was coming easier already. "Lawrence will look after me, don't worry. Dearest Keira, you need to check on your friend. I'm worried about Gwen."

"GM, she's at work! It's not even lunchtime!"

"No, Keira… it's well past noon," she sighed. "This has happened before. Look at your watch."

I held my watch up. It read 4:15 pm.

Oh shit.

TWENTY FIVE

My car skidded as I turned into her driveway. As soon as it came to a stop I leapt over the door and sprinted up the driveway, past her truck to the front door.

With any luck she'd be fine and I'd use the excuse of checking in to see how she had liked dinner with Lawrence and GM

Devon was on the front porch, the magazine he'd been reading spread on his thighs while his head lolled to the side, sound asleep, snoring. Buster must have seen me coming; he was cowering over at the farthest end of the porch. I didn't want to wake Devon, so I crept around him and through the front door.

I stepped inside and listened for any sound of activity, where Gwen might be found. When I walked across the hall and paused at the foot of the long staircase, her voice drifted down. Okay, she's on the phone or something—that was a good sign.

As I tiptoed up the stairs I could hear her voice.

"Can you hear me?" came from her half open room door. "Are you there Mom?"

"Gwen?" I said when I got to the doorway.

"AAAGH!" she cried out. I burst into the room. She was on her feet, her eyes wide, while her hand swept up to her neck before she breathed a sigh. "Oh, it's you, Keira." She glanced away, blushing.

"Yeah. Sorry. The door was open and your dad is asleep on the veranda. I should have—"

"No! It's fine." Her hand fell and she clasped my arm. "Maybe you can help me!"

She pulled me into her room and I stopped short, seeing what was on the bed. Oh my God. Not a Ouija board. This was too much!

"What the hell are you doing with *that*?" I said, pointing at it.

Her eyes glinted with excitement and she tucked a stray lock of hair behind her ear, before she pulled me over to the bed. "I'm trying to contact my mother! You know how you said you saw her, well, I thought with a little help from this, I might be able to as well!"

I shook my head. "No Gwen. You don't want to mess with that thing."

Her fingers dug into my arm. "Come on, Keira. Please. I just know if you do it with me, I'll get to talk to my mother. I mean, you've got some kind of gift or something. I believed you when you said you saw her! Hell, I've always felt her nearby."

"No Gwen! Look these Ouija boards are bad news!" If she knew what I'd seen earlier, she'd burn the bloody thing! "Not going to happen, Gwen!" I started to fold the board up to put it back in its box.

Her hand tugged mine away and she glared at me. "You're being selfish. All I want is a chance to—"

"Gwen! Believe me when I tell you this is *dangerous*! You don't want to mess with it." I jerked my hand away from hers.

"Hey!" Her eyes started to glisten again, but this time it was with tears. "It's my *mother* we're talking about. She would never hurt me."

"This is *so* not a good idea, Gwen. Just trust me when I tell you your mother is fine." If GM knew this was going on, that Gwen was trying to get me to do this with her, she'd have a conniption! Hell, even Lawrence would blow a gasket! And the coincidence was totally freaking me out!

"Please. I just want to speak with her...just one more time. I've missed her so much! I promise, I'll never ask you again. Just one time...please." Her voice almost broke when she pleaded. She swiped the tears away with the back of her hand and sniffed loudly.

She still had her hand on my arm. The sorrow and grief I felt from her dad was nothing compared to the agony in Gwen's heart. Damn it. I took a deep breath and knew I couldn't deny her this. If it was my last time seeing my mother or father....or even GM, I'd want to do it. "Fine! But this is it. I'll only do this once." I flopped down on the bed, next to the blasted board. I glared up at her. "But blow your nose first."

She rose to her tiptoes, holding her hands tight to her chest, almost squee'ing. I swear if she did that, I was out of there. When she flew from the room to get a tissue, I glared at the board and planchette. *No tricks this time buster.*

All too soon she was back and bouncing to a spot opposite me, with the board between us.

"Have you used one of these things before?" Her fingers flew to the planchette and she looked over at me.

I rolled my eyes and my hands slowly drifted over to join hers on the small triangle. "Oh yeah. Have you? I mean aside from just now?"

"No. I just bought it today. I was thinking of what happened the other day by the pool and I was right outside some kind of mystical head shop downtown. I went right in and bought it."

"Right about 9:00 am or so?" that was when GM and I started our session. Yeah, the one that took five minutes but lasted seven hours. I had such a bad feeling about this.

"Yeah! I was on my break! How did you know?"

"Skip it. Let's give this a whirl, then I'm going to burn this thing, okay?" Great. She just happened to be outside the right store at the right minute. Sure. Just coincidence. I didn't believe in coincidences. Well, this would be a quick down and dirty session and then I was done with the Ouija board. "You'd better let me do the talking."

Her face knotted. "Why? It's *my* mother and *my* board."

I lifted my hands from the planchette and sat back. "My rules. If you want me to do this with you, you'll do it my way or forget it." I'd been trained by an expert after all, while she was a neophyte.

Her eyebrows clenched in annoyance. "Okay." It came out like a bark.

I took a few deep breaths and then my hands went back to the board. A flash of Gwen's mom appeared in my head. This was a good start. My eyes opened wider and I peered at Gwen. "What's your mom's name?"

"Rebecca. Rebecca Jones but her maiden name was Dowd."

I took a deep breath and started. "Rebecca Jones. Are you here?"

The planchette sat still, no vibrations, nothing.

"Rebecca Dowd. Your daughter Gwen would like to talk to you. Are you present?" This time the triangle jerked to the word, 'Yes'. I glanced at Gwen and was rewarded by a smile.

"Ask her if she's happy. Tell her I miss her."

It was all I could do not to roll my eyes. As if, Rebecca wouldn't have heard that! "Rebecca, Gwen would like a sign that you are in peace and that you are happy."

My fingertips on the planchette began to tingle and it was hard to stay on the small object as it spelled out, 'Love her.'

"Oh Mom." A single tear splashed onto the board from Gwen's chin.

The planchette began to circle the board, gaining speed. My eyes darted to Gwen who stared back at me, her mouth hung open.

The triangle stopped at the letters 'J A R R O D'.

"Uh oh," I said. My heart galloped against my rib cage. The air became cooler and a sudden breeze lifted the curtain from the side of the window. The loose paper on the desk began to lift and swirl in the air.

Gwen's eyes were as big as dinner plates staring around the room. Her hands drifted off the zooming planchette and I reached to slap them back on, holding my palm over the tops of her hands. Fear and despair came in crashing waves from where we joined. This was so unfair! Gwen had hoped for contact from her mother and this thing...whatever it was, was hijacking that.

"Listen shithead! Whoever you are...Jarrod or some other weasely shmuck, get lost!" The triangle began to circle the board so fast it was hard to keep my fingers on it. I was making it mad.

On a roll now, I continued, "You sneaky coward! Taking advantage of the love between Gwen and her mother! You have no place in this house!"

The bedroom door banged shut with such force it shook the room that was already swirling with papers. Gwen's arms jerked back and I gripped her hand in mine. "Stay connected, Gwen! I need you to stay with me here!" Fear jolted into my hand from hers and then became a steady, calm strength. I looked into her eyes and saw determination narrow her gaze.

"I command you to leave this house! You have no right to be here!" My fingers laced with Gwen's and we held our hands up, still maintaining the connection with the planchette with our other hands. Books on her bookshelf toppled to the floor. The wind became wilder, forcing the papers against our hands and faces.

My head filled with a face, the eyes red while the mouth gaped in a grin...an evil grin that taunted me.

Oh screw you, buster. I raised my voice. "ENOUGH! GO!"

Our hands tightened, and our muscles were taut when we raised our arms even higher. Just as suddenly as it started, the room became quiet. Papers floated in the still air and drifted onto the bed and floor around us. We looked at each other and then our gaze shifted to take in the room. It had worked! Together we'd done it!

"Oh my God! What happened?" Gwen's mouth fell open as she leaned closer to me. Her hand left the planchette and gripped my arm. "Jarrod's the name of the guy found dead in your grandmother's house I was talking about! Keira, what's going on?"

Good question. But more like, what the hell was he doing here, in Gwen's house? It was as unlikely as seeing Gwen's name spelled out in the session with GM. I gasped. This was all a diversion! Of course I would be concerned after seeing her name and would come over to check on her. And then, for her to *conveniently* buy a Ouija board that day and try this? I was meant to be here—the message on the board, and the room exploding with a sudden wind!

GM! This was all to get me out of the house so GM would be alone! Lawrence was old and had no power! I jumped to my feet. "I've got to go! My Nana's in danger! I'll explain later!"

This time, my feet thundered on the stairs as I rushed down and out the door. Devon lifted his head and called out to me, "Keira? What the devil?" The dog took this opportunity, seeing me racing from the yard, to howl like a hyena.

The tires of my car skidded on the shoulder of the road as I raced home. GM had said demons lie and try to trick you. Whatever that thing was that screwed us over back at the house had set us up. Set *me* up.

I had to get there! Had to get to G.M before it was too late! Tears filled my eyes and the entrance to the driveway was a blur. Was I already too late?

"Nana!" I sobbed.

TWENTY SIX

I burst through the front door of Nana's home and almost keeled over from the putrid stench in the house. The vision of half gnawed, bloated carcasses covered in their own filth burst into my mind's eye. For the first time in my life I knew the smell of pure evil. I retched twice, and stood upright, and spoke aloud as I staggered through the house to Nana's bedroom:

> *"I will not be afraid*
> *Fear is the soul destroyer*
> *And will consume me should I allow it*
> *I rebuke fear*
> *To its face of many masks I stare unafraid*
> *One by one, I will watch those masks fall away*
> *Crumble to ash*
> *And drift away*
> *In the breeze of my love*
> *And I will still stand*
> *Alone and unafraid."*

It really didn't help much; I was still scared to death. But I kept trudging, each step an effort. The stench had a physical aspect to it—a morass that thickened, as I moved forward.

"I rebuke fear," I said, over and over.

I was halfway across the living room when I heard Nana's terrified scream, followed by the sound of a body slamming so hard the floor under my feet vibrated. I dropped my head and charged as another wail from Nana stabbed my ears.

Coming through the shattered door to her bedroom I gasped. GM's body hovered two feet above the bed! She clung to the headboard, as her legs were being twisted and yanked. Her hair streamed down and her eyes were wide with terror.

A mighty wind howled through the room.

"Nana!" I rushed forward. The force that held her, slammed her to the bed.

And turned on me.

I was lifted a foot off the floor and flung back against the doorjamb. I fell like a rag doll, the impact dazing me. I saw Lawrence slumped against the far wall. He was out cold, blood streaking his forehead.

Nana's body began to rise again and I scrambled to my feet.

"Keira, go back!" she cried out. She clawed again at the headboard, clutching a bedpost as the rest of her body was twisted and pulled.

"Leave her alone!" I bolted to the bed, this time almost making it before I was flung back onto my ass again. The demon's grip on Nana faltered and she dropped again to the bed.

I got up again. It couldn't levitate her and defend against me at the same time.

"OH YOU THINK SO, MEATBAG?' screamed in my mind. The room was blotted from my vision, and filled with a gaping, drooling maw of broken brown teeth. Its tongue pulsed out and I leapt back to keep from being swabbed by it rancidness.

HAHAHAHA!

It vanished, and another pulse of force knocked me to my knees. The pain of the blow was excruciating. I was on all fours, gasping for breath as Nana was again yanked off the bed, and slammed back down. The demon was trying to pull away from her mattress and over the hardwood floor, but she was hanging onto the bedpost for dear life.

I pushed myself to my feet, my body wracked in pain.

"Keira!" It came from behind me.

I turned and saw Gwen! But then I was once more flat on the floor, the wind knocked out of me. A loud thud and Nana's scream broke through my dazed head.

Gwen's hands gripped my arm, tugging me to my feet. "Keira! Your grandmother!" She held me upright, her arm around my waist.

When Gwen grasped me, a dynamic surge coursed through every cell in my body. I felt strengthened in a way I'd never experienced before; a balloon within me I didn't even know I had swelled and burst forth.

"LEAVE THIS HOUSE, BEAST!" I screamed. The thunder that exploded from my throat shook the room. "I REBUKE YOU! I COMMAND YOU, GO!"

Nana dropped onto her bed and instantly, the room was normal. The disgusting stench vanished and the howling wind stopped like a light switch was thrown. I was immediately woozy, and staggered. I would have fallen right on my face if Gwen hadn't caught me. We lurched over to the bed.

Nana was flat on her back and her eyes were closed, her hands no longer clasping the headboard. I bent over her, stroking her cheek.

"Nana?" I burst into tears, sobbing. "Nana?" Oh God, she was so small and so still.

Gwen reached around me with one arm and began to shake Nana; her other one still wrapped around my waist. "Pamela!" she shouted. "Pamela, wake up!"

Her eyelids fluttered and creaked open.

"Keira." It was a whispered sigh from her lips. I dropped to my knees on the floor beside her and held my arm over her, now bawling like a child. "Oh Nana! I shouldn't have left! That *beast* tricked me!"

Gwen's hand gripped my shoulder. "What the hell *was* that thing?"

It was then that it hit me. I hadn't been able to beat the thing back on my own. It had taken Gwen's presence, joining with me that had given me the supercharge. If she hadn't shown up when she did...God, I couldn't bear to think of it. Tears rolled down my cheeks and onto Nana's bed. We'd probably all be dead if she hadn't shown up.

"Lawrence!" Just as the thought had popped into my head, Gwen noticed him. She raced over to the far wall and squatted next to him. Her fingers checked his neck for a pulse and then she looked over at me, letting out an audible sigh of relief. "He's alive!" Like she did with Nana, Gwen prodded Lawrence. "Hey, Lawrence! Wake up! What's for supper?"

His eyes opened slowly and he pushed himself up, staring at Gwen and then turning to see my grandmother. He started to get to his feet, "Pamela!"

"She's okay, Lawrence. Well, bruised and shaken up, but she's okay!" I brushed the tears from my eyes and turned back to gaze down at my Nana. Nana. Yeah, she was all of that. No more GM "I'll call an ambulance. We need to get you to the hospital to check you out. Lawrence as well." I stroked her cheek with the back of my hand.

She shook her head. "That's not necessary. But, I do need some water."

I didn't want to leave her, but I rose to my feet.

"I got this," I said. Lawrence could probably use one too. In a flash, I was back from the kitchen carrying two glasses of water. Nana had managed to prop a pillow behind her and was sitting up. She was a tough old bird, that was for sure. Even so, her hand trembled as she took the glass.

Lawrence was seated at the foot of the bed. He waved off the offer of water and was staring at Nana. "Pamela, I'm sorry. I failed you." Reaching up to her, his hand cupped her cheek while his eyes welled with tears.

"You could never fail me, dear." She looked up at Gwen and me. "But the torch must pass to younger hands."

TWENTY SEVEN

G wen folded her arms over her chest, her gaze darting over each of us. "For the record, I think you should get checked by a doctor. While we're there, I'm getting a CAT scan because I've just lost my mind." She looked around the room, her eyes widening. "What the hell just happened here?"

Nana looked up at me and smiled. "I think you were right about Gwen. She will do nicely."

"I agree." Lawrence took the glass of water from me and gulped half of it down. He made a face and he smirked looking at the glass. "I think brandy would be better, y'know." The hair on his head was sticking out all over the place.

Gwen's fingers threaded through her hair and fisted. "I'm standing right here, by the way. Will someone please tell me what's going on?" She scowled at me and her hands dropped hard at her sides.

"Gwen. I don't know where to begin." It was true. How would I ever explain it rationally? The Veil? Demons? Spirits being transitioned? *Mind reading?* I'd been involved with all this for a week now and I couldn't believe what had just happened.

"How about you start by telling me what was attacking your grandmother? Was it the same thing that was in my bedroom before, when we did the Ouija board?"

"Keira! Tell me you didn't use the Ouija board with Gwen!" Nana sat forward, wincing as her weight settled on her hips.

"That's it, isn't it! I'm right! That same thing, that demon or ghost or whatever it was, attacked your grandmother."

"Now who's talking like I'm not here?" Nana muttered and took another sip of water. "You're right, Lawrence. This calls for brandy."

When Lawrence turned to leave, I held up my hand stopping him."You sit down. Everyone, just chill for a minute, will you! I'll get the brandy. A round for all of us." I called over my shoulder as I headed out, "Gwen grab a chair. This is going to take a while."

I set the full decanter on a tray along with four snifters and winced a little at the aches all over my body. I was going to be plenty sore tomorrow.

I marched back into Nana's room...Nana's room. I smiled. That felt right saying it, even if it was just in my head.

Gwen had pulled the upholstered chair close to the bed, while Lawrence nestled on the bed next to Nana. I set the tray on her nightstand and poured.

After Nana had hers in hand, I extended Lawrence his glass. He smiled up at me. "This is nice. Me being served for a change. I could get used to this."

I smiled and shook my head. "Anytime, Lawrence." When Gwen and I each had our glasses, I pulled up the chair from the dressing table and took a seat. I turned to Gwen, who was still looking suspiciously at the rest of us. "First of all, I want to thank you for helping me earlier. If you hadn't shown up when you did...Wait a minute. Why did you?"

Gwen's jaw tightened. "Oh for Pete's sake! I'm the one who gets to ask the questions. But for your information, the way you tore out of my house, I knew there was trouble. I knew I had to help you."

"A very good sign, wouldn't you say, Pamela?" Lawrence smiled and nudged Nana with his hand.

"Very." She took a sip of the liquor and sighed, folding her hand over his.

I had to bite my cheeks to keep from laughing at the exasperation on Gwen's face. Before she could start yelling again, I took a deep breath. "It was a demon that was in your bedroom. I caught a flash of it there and realized its plot. The Ouija board, you buying it...it was all a set-up. A diversion. The real target was my grandmother."

She leaned forward, her hand gripping her knee. "But why? Why would that thing, want to hurt her?"

"It was the work of my enemy. I don't doubt that. But that brings up the real danger. Now that that demon knows about you Keira, no doubt *my enemy* does too." Nana's eyes were steely, gazing over at me.

"Again, you're talking in riddles. Can someone just explain what's going on here in plain language?" Gwen's fingers thrummed on her leg.

Lawrence sat forward. "For years Pamela has worked with the spirit world, Gwen. She can see and communicate with them. She has helped many people; done work at hospitals, prisons and, well anyplace where spirits linger. She convinces them to move on...to go to the higher plane where they should be."

Gwen's mouth slowly drifted open and her eyes gaped at him. "She can communicate with the dead?" She turned to me. "Like you?"

"Actually, I've only been doing it since I arrived here last week." I tilted my head. "Nana's been doing it for years and years."

Nana leaned forward. "Gwen, I do this to help people and spirits find peace. For the most part neither are comfortable when they inhabit the same space in the earthly plane. There is a thin Veil that separates life and death. When the souls of those who've died refuse to pass through...either from fear or confusion—"

"Or love." Gwen was thinking of her mother.

Nana nodded. "Yes, that's a powerful motivation to linger." She took a breath and continued, "But there is a natural progression of existence. Spirits are meant to move on. Too much of their energy on this plane damages the natural order. It even impacts the universe."

"Kind of like the butterfly effect." Gwen's eyebrows formed a V. "I've studied physics and even became familiar with Quantum physics." She held up her hand. "Wait. No. You're talking about stuff String Theory touches on, aren't you? A multi-dimensional model of existence."

"I can't speak to the technical aspects, it's more an intuitive thing for me. I just know that The Veil becomes weaker because of this."

"But why would anyone want to interfere with this process, the natural order of things? What is to be *gained* if this veil becomes weak?" Gwen's eyes narrowed, trying to process this.

Lawrence sighed. "Sometimes, there isn't a *specific* gain for people to act the way they do. Chaos, a breakdown of order is a sufficient goal, in and of itself. Think of it like these computer hackers creating viruses and malware. They gain nothing but the thrill of creating havoc in other people's lives."

I watched her closely to see how this was all going down with her. She had a grasp of it but would she be willing to devote her life like Lawrence had? "Gwen? You and I were meant to work together on this. When we joined hands, the power to fight off that entity went off the charts."

She held up her hand cutting me off. "Hold on! There're a lot more questions I want answers to. First of all...what's with this *house*? The place has been haunted for years and yet you, Mrs. York, some kind of ghost buster, lived with it? How could you stay here? How could *they*, if this has been your life's work?"

Nana smiled and took a sip of her brandy, totally unfazed by Gwen's questions. "I bought this house *because* it was haunted. But it wasn't just that it was haunted—it sits on an axis of supernatural power, a Ley line."

"A what?"

"Ley lines. Corridors of power that transcends the world as we know it. Some of the better known Ley line axes are Stonehenge, the Mayan temples and the pyramids but there are many grid lines that cross the earth. This house sits on the axis of two powerful ones."

Nana smiled and rested a hand on Gwen's forearm. "As for the ghosts that have lived here...most of them, I dispelled. I kept a few for training purposes, yes." She glanced over to me. "But it was more than that, Keira. Molly and Sam became old friends; believe it or not, I miss them now." She turned her head to Gwen. "So I can appreciate you wanting your mother's sprit to linger."

"Thank you," she replied.

"But dear, it comes at a cost. She's not where she belongs."

Gwen's eyes narrowed. "I'll be the judge of that."

They did a sort of stare down. Without looking away, Nana said softly, "No, Gwen; that decision will rest with your mother." She blinked. "That's a topic for another day, I think. I was talking about the spirits that stayed on here until Keira arrived."

"Yeah," I said. "You kept Jerrod on to show me how tough it can be. Did you know about the demon all this time?"

"No. It had never shown itself. I had used the Ouija board to force Jerrod's hand; but as I told you, using it risks opening a channel for those beasts." She turned to Gwen, "As you saw for yourself." Gwen stayed silent. "It was necessary for Keira to see that this vocation has its risks."

"Well, you sure demonstrated that!" I said. This time it was my turn to be confused. "But Jarrod...he's still here, right? I'm pretty sure the demon was holding him here. Jarrod was too frightened by it to make any sort of move."

Nana turned to me. "I believe Jarrod moved on when you vanquished the demon here. By that time, after being in its thrall, he was quite ready to go."

"How did I get the demon to leave? I did it at Gwen's as

well, even though I still think it was a set-up from the get go."

Nana looked from me, to Gwen and back, chewing her lower lip. "Because of Gwen, I think. Together, both of you were strong enough to push it back. But don't make the mistake of thinking you've destroyed it. It's regrouping even as we speak. Although it will need some time for that. Just as we are bruised from our battle, so is it. Nana held her glass out for a refill. "That is good brandy. It's hitting the spot, all right."

I topped her up and then downed some of my own glass, relishing the burn as it made its way down my throat. I felt the warmth extend right into my bones. I rolled my shoulders, wincing at the pain.

Gwen wasn't giving up with the questions "The rose in your front yard...it blooms even in winter. Is that part of this Ley line thing? The house sitting on kind of hallowed ground or power grid?"

"Yes, you're on the right track," Nana chuckled. "There is tremendous power here. Whenever I've been abroad, doing my work, I come home drained. It takes a lot out of you, as you will find out, Keira. This house itself recharges me. It's been a solace that I searched the world to find. It helps that's it's not terribly far from where my daughter lives, as well."

I took a deep breath. It was do or die time. "Gwen, would you consider helping me with continuing what my grandmother has done?"

Her eyes opened wide. "Are you kidding me? This would be the dream come true! It would be fascinating!" She looked around the room. "Even if it gets scary." She closed her eyes and shook her head. "But I can't. I have my father to look after, not to mention my job. I can't go traipsing around the world with you."

I scoffed and my hand fluttered high dismissing her concerns. "Don't worry about your dad. I'll hire the very best care and as for your job...*really*? I'll pay you a *lot* more than what you're making at the Post Office. We'll make a great team!" I slapped her knee.

She shook her head. "It's not about money. My big concern

is my dad. From the sounds of it, we'd be gone for long periods of time. I'm not sure about that part."

"Look Gwen, we can figure something out. I think the important question right now, is if you would want to do this work. I think you do. I really like your dad and he'd want you to be happy, wouldn't he? We won't abandon him, don't worry." I knew we could do this, together.

I looked over at Lawrence and Nana who were holding hands, smiling at us. She let go of his hand and held out her hands to us. "Take my hands, girls."

The three of us, held hands, making a small circle. I felt in my heart what I can only describe as a rose colored glow fill and spread out through my chest. Gwen let out a little gasp, and Nana smiled.

She let go and looked at us with a knowing smile. "You two are Kindred Spirits you know."

Gwen chuckled. "I was thinking the same thing." She turned her head to me, nodding.

"Kindred Spirits, huh? I like that term. It sounds cool."

Gwen and Nana looked at each other and laughed. What was so funny? I shrugged. Let them have their private joke. "Anyone care for some key lime pie?"

TWENTY EIGHT

Gwen followed me into the kitchen. "I'm still smoked by what just happened. All this time, your grandmother and Lawrence have been living this secret life— travelling the world and being some kind of exorcist or something. Confronting demons even!"

I popped the frozen pie into the microwave to thaw and then turned to her. "When he started, Lawrence didn't have any special abilities in this. He trained himself to become attuned to it, so he could help my grandmother."

"Well, I've never *seen* my dead mother...but I've sensed her being near, if that counts for anything." Gwen reached for the plates and set them down on the counter. "And I've read a lot about this, so that gives me a leg up, I think."

My arm curled over her shoulder. "You don't have to sell me on you, Gwen. If you hadn't shown up, this would have gone badly. I know that. And it was when we held hands in your bedroom that whatever power I have, got amplified. And here, the same thing happened." I squeezed her shoulder. "I think you've got it, whatever 'it' is!"

Her smile fell and she stepped away. "But my mother...by your grandmother's logic, she should move on. Call me selfish, but I hate the thought of that."

I blew out a long sigh, looking down at the floor. "I can understand that. Your dad gets comfort out of her being near as well. None of you are ready to part from each other. There will come a time, but not yet." I turned when the microwave beeped and opened the door. "There're lots of spirits who stay for bad reasons—fear, confusion, anger. I'd say they're the ones who need to be convinced to leave."

"So, this enemy of your grandmother's...who is it? Do you know? She seemed to think that this demon, Jarrod or whatever was working with him."

I stared at her. "I'm pretty sure it's my grandfather. His name is David Holmes. Lawrence warned me to forget about him. But I think, knowing your enemy is the first step in the battle. And now that Nana—"

"You're calling her *Nana* now, not GM?" Gwen grinned. "That's progress."

"Yeah." My cheeks warmed and I smiled back at her. "Anyway...now that Nana thinks he knows about me, the stakes just got higher. If that thing that was in the bedroom is somehow allied with him, he must have some paranormal ability himself, like Nana. It probably explains how they got together, even if it was short lived."

She was quiet as we dished out the pie and put it on a tray. Finally she spoke."How much of this can I tell my father? If I do take you up doing this, I've got to tell him something. And I might have an answer to nursing care for him."

My heart leapt and I grinned. She was actually going to do this! I'd liked her right from the start and we'd make a good team. "What's that?"

She grinned. "His sister, Elizabeth. She's retiring from nursing this year. It might not be too hard to convince her to retire here. He's the only family she's got. I'm not her biggest fan, nor is she mine. She's a bit of a busybody."

"But does *he* get along with her?"

"Dad gets along with everyone. Even her."

"Well, there's no rush in this. I probably have much to learn from Nana...and Lawrence could give you lots of pointers, I'm sure." I was about to pick up the tray but she nudged me away. "I'll get this." She snorted. "Just call me, Lawrence."

"Never! He can be stodgy. I'd never accuse you of that!" I followed her from the kitchen and back to my grandmother's room. I almost ran into her when she stopped short in the doorway.

She stepped to the side and nodded with her head for me to check out the room. They were both sound asleep, snuggled together. It was such a sweet picture with Nana's head on Lawrence's chest, his arm around her, holding her close. They had a deep history and obvious love for each other.

I backed out of the room and turned the light off, leaving only the lamp on the bed side table lit. It had been a day from hell and they deserved to rest.

TWENTY NINE

Gwen and I had spent most of that evening chatting and getting to know each other better. When she left, I locked up and got caught up, sending emails to my mother and replying to one from Cerise, who was anxious for me to return home. She missed our nights partying at the clubs. It was funny. The thought of going back to that held no appeal. I drummed my fingers on my desktop. Cerise was the only one of the group of friends I had in New York who contacted me; the others couldn't care less if I fell of the face of the earth.

But then... I felt pretty much the same about them. I had never really fit in with a group of friends. I was always the one standing right at the edge of being an outsider.

***

When I woke up, the day was overcast and threatening rain again. I was about to roll over and catch forty more winks but a feeling of dread settled in my gut. It could have been some sort of hang-over from yesterday, but I didn't think so. I lay there for a couple of minutes until I couldn't stand it anymore.

Something was wrong.

I threw my robe on and hustled over to the stairwell. As I passed Lawrence's room, seeing the door closed, I wondered if he had managed to get up to bed or if he'd spent the night with my grandmother. They'd been out cold when Gwen and I went in there, which considering the attack on both of them, was understandable.

The kitchen was empty with no sign of Lawrence. No smell of coffee and the pot was still off. Shaking my head, I stepped over to it and got it going. After flipping the switch I strode out to the sun room. That's where she normally had breakfast. But again, it was empty, with the first splatters of rain hitting the glass dome overhead.

Well, this was going to be awkward...going into my grandmother's room to get them up! I knocked on the door. "Nana? Lawrence?" Silence was the only answer.

The feeling of dread sank lower in my gut. I turned the handle and opened the door wide enough to peek inside. The bed covers were rumpled from the night they'd spent there but otherwise it was empty. Where were they?

I raced to the front door. Maybe they were more seriously hurt than we'd thought and Lawrence had taken Nana to the hospital or something. But wouldn't they have told me? When I spied the black Cadillac next to my rental car, it was like a punch to the stomach. I spun around, looking up the staircase to the upper floors. "Nana?" This time, my voice yelled loudly. "Lawrence?"

The living room. I darted through the door and peered around. Again, no sign of them. I was running by this time, going from the dining room, to the downstairs bath, up the stairs and calling out to them all the while. My voice echoed in the hallway and I jerked the door of Lawrence's room wide. His bed was made and everything was in order, exactly as I would have thought for someone like him, even if I'd never been in there before.

My heart raced along with my feet as I ran down the hallway, throwing every door open and peering inside the rooms. They weren't here! I raced across to the window, and scanned the yard. There was no sign of them.

Had they called a taxi and gone off somewhere? Maybe there was a note that I'd overlooked. I raced back downstairs, glancing at the table near the door and striding through the dining room. Nothing there. I burst through the door to the kitchen, my gaze darting from the counter to the fridge where a grocery list hung. Nothing. The table was clear as well.

I turned quickly at the gurgling of the coffee pot as the last of the water seeped through. This was weird. I took a deep breath and forced myself to pour a mug. There had to be some explanation for them not being there. They wouldn't just up and leave me, would they? I couldn't see Nana doing that. Did it have something to do with what happened last night? That somehow her enemy had kidnapped them or something? But I would have heard if there'd been any kind of commotion.

I set the mug down and once more my feet were flying to my grandmother's room. It was a total shot in the dark, but I barged into the bathroom adjoining her room. The room was pristine from the neatly arranged towels to the gleaming porcelain tub.

Back in my grandmother's bedroom, I looked around, searching for any clue as to why both she and Lawrence were gone. It was then that I noticed the envelope on her dressing table, propped up against the mirror. I sprinted over and picked it up. It was my grandmother's writing, with my name on the front.

My fingers trembled tearing the flap open, tugging the letter out and the smell of roses wafted up.

Dear Keira,
Let me begin by telling you how much I love you and how proud of you, I am. The fact that you are reading this letter, means that I am gone.

I shall miss our daily chats and watching you blossom, delighting in discovering the gifts which are my legacy to you. It was much too short a time together, a fact that now, I deeply regret. There are photo albums in my night stand. They're filled with pictures of you— from when you were born to just earlier this year. They don't do you justice, Keira. They don't reveal the jewel inside that you truly are. Oh, to have known you when you were growing up!

All my worldly goods are now yours, along with my undying love. Use them wisely, as well as your talents in following my life's work. It is good work. It's IMPORTANT work and I've never regretted it for one minute. You will do me proud, when you continue with it, I am sure!

Take care, my dear and know that I'll always love you!
All my love, for all time,
Your Nana.

She'd left? Where would she have gone? There was no clue in anything she'd written.

I walked over to her closet and opened the sliding door. Dresses and tops hung from hangers and the shoe rack was jammed to bordering an overflow. If she'd taken off travelling, she was travelling light.

My eyes popped open wide. Mom! Maybe she knew where Nana was. I raced up the stairs and into my bedroom. I grabbed my cell phone when I saw a waiting text message from my father. It had just come in.

We just heard and we're on our way. We'll be in Kingston as soon as we can. Stay put. We'll take a cab from the airport.

Heard what? My heart did a nosedive into my belly. Whatever they'd heard, the fact that both my parents were coming to Kingston was not good. I tried calling them, only to be told on both their cells phones that the call could not be completed. My fingers flew replying to Dad's text. I watched the small screen for a few minutes but no reply came through.

The feeling of dread I'd awoken with was now alarm. There was something wrong. Nana was gone and I had no idea where.

I started crying. That letter was a goodbye.

THIRTY

I moved like a zombie going through the motions of showering and getting dressed. I glanced outside before trudging down the stairs. It was a steady rain, from a dull gray sky. The house was so quiet, the storm was a white noise against the roof and windows.

As I was about to pass through the foyer to get a cup of coffee, there was a pounding at the front door. My heart skipped a beat as I raced over to answer it. They were back!

When I opened the door and saw Gwen, my shoulders fell. "Oh. Hi. Come in."

She didn't smile as she stepped inside, already unzipping the yellow slicker and throwing the hood back. It only just then occurred to me. Why wasn't she at work? The mail must go through and all that. She reached in her pocket and withdrew an envelope.

"I'm sorry. I would have come sooner but I had to get someone to cover my route." She withdrew a letter and handed it to me. "This was in my truck this morning. It's from Lawrence."

I read it.

Dear Gwen,

I was wrong about my first impressions that you were not suitable to take up the mantle of Guardian. That's what I have been to Pamela for these many years and now, after what happened last night, I see that you are true and able to continue in that role with Keira.

If I had any words of wisdom to depart to you, it is this, trust your intuition. That silent inner voice has proved itself many times, saving Pamela and I on many occasions. Even if Keira, who can be headstrong and impulsive, wants to rush headfirst into a 'situation', if your gut is telling you otherwise, trust it.

Good luck to you! I know you will do well with Keira. Even though Pamela and I are gone, our hearts and best wishes are with you. Please, when you read this letter, go to Keira. She will be receiving instructions later this day. It's important that you are there for her.

With Warmest Regards,
Lawrence

I stared at Gwen. "This is like the letter that Nana left for me! And my parents are on their way here! What do you make of all this?"

She shook her head. "I got a bad feeling when I read his letter. Let me see what your grandmother wrote."

We hurried into the bedroom and I handed her the letter, watching her as she read it. The bad feeling I'd had before just got worse.

She looked up and her eyes were wide staring at me when she finished reading. "They are definitely gone." She stared at me until her gaze faltered. "I hate to even say this, but do you think that something bad happened to them? That maybe they're..."

Oh God. My knees turned to rubber and I gripped the table to keep from falling over. It was the thing that I didn't want to even think about...but I already had. Hearing her almost say the word was still a punch in the gut. "I don't know. But the fact that my parents...." I couldn't finish. My chin quivered and hot tears sprang to my eyes.

Gwen stepped forward and took me in her arms. We stood holding each other while I cried. "It can't be, Gwen. There's got to be an explanation. She's gone away on a trip somewhere." I pulled back and my heart took a leap of faith. "Maybe the airport. We could contact them to see if they took a flight somewhere?"

She sighed. "Yeah. We could do that. But first let's go to the kitchen. We'll have a coffee and figure this out." As we walked from the bedroom, her arm still around my shoulders, she continued. "It doesn't sound like your grandmother, though. To just up and leave in the middle of the night? She hardly left this house...ever."

I sniffed and then looked up at her. "And her clothes. It doesn't look like she packed anything. You don't suppose that my grandfather has something to do with this do you?"

She steered me to the table. "Sit down. I'll get the coffee." As she poured it, she glanced over at me. "I don't know why, but it doesn't feel like that to me. And your grandmother said that whatever that thing was, it needed time to regroup...get its strength back."

I had to agree with her. My instincts were that this had nothing to do with him. The letters were too nice; I didn't pick up any hint of coercion from them. And the fact that Lawrence's letter asked Gwen to come over to be with me...

I felt the blood drain from my face. "Gwen, they *planned* this!"

"What? How?"

"I don't know! But my Dad 'heard'!" I held up my cell phone for her to read the message. I tried calling him again, with no luck, and he hadn't replied to my text from earlier.

We had no choice but to sit tight and wait.

***

"Hello?" It was my mother's voice at the front door. I got up from the chair in the greenhouse, leaving Gwen still poring over the photo album. I raced to the foyer, where Dad was setting their bags on the floor. Mom looked at me with red rimmed eyes and her nose was pink set against a pale blotchy complexion. She'd been crying. At the sight, tears sprang to my eyes too and I let myself be pulled into her embrace.

When Dad's arms circled both of us, I knew that whatever happened with Nana, I'd never see her again.

The thought just made me cry harder. I felt so empty without her. It was unfair that I'd just got to know my grandmother and she was gone. Feeling my mother's sobs, I could only imagine how devastated she had to be feeling. We stood like that for a while, each of us trying to comfort each other.

My dad's voice broke through. "Who are you?"

I pulled back from Mom and looked to where he was staring. Gwen stood there in her Postie uniform with her hands clasped together above her tummy. Her eyes were wide and also full of tears. She wiped her cheek with her hand and strode forward, squaring her shoulders. "Hi Mr. Swanson, Mrs. Swanson. I'm Gwen, a friend of Keira's."

My father broke away and took her hand, shaking it and then covering both their hands with his other one. "Please, it's Richard. Nice to meet you, Gwen."

Mom stretched out her hand. "I'm Susan. Pleased to meet you. I'm glad you've kept Keira company while she waited here for us." She folded Gwen into a hug and patted her back. Stepping back, she held Gwen by her shoulders. "Are you Keira's Guardian?"

Gwen didn't hesitate a second. "Yes," she said, nodding.

Mom and Dad glanced at one another. "What's going on, Dad? What did you hear about Nana's disappearance? Where is she?" I could barely get the words out. My lips quivered and my throat was taut fighting back the tears.

He sighed. "Oh Keira. My poor baby girl." He put his arm around me and hugged me.

Mom's hand lifted to rub my back. "She's gone, Keira. She has been for a couple of weeks. Both she and Lawrence—"

"No! She was here!" I spun around to face her. "What are you talking about? She was here last night! I've spent the week with her!"

"Honey, no." Dad spoke up. "She died two weeks ago. As did Lawrence."

What the hell were they talking about? My head swiveled to Gwen. "Tell them Gwen! You were here. Nana and Lawrence are alive. They were here!"

"She's right, Richard. The four of us were together last night!" Her eyes were so big they threatened to pop right out onto her cheeks.

"Keira. It's time you found out the truth. It's a long story. Mr. Thompson will be here shortly and I've no wish for him to witness our family secrets. Let's go in the kitchen and have a coffee while I explain." My mother's eyes were still welling but her chin lifted and she started across the foyer.

My knees were like spaghetti noodles and it was hard to breathe. What the hell was my mother talking about? A family secret? She was wrong! Nana and Lawrence had just gone away. They'd been there...had dinner with us...even fought the demon thing last night. What was happening with my parents? Had they lost their minds?

Dad forced a small smile at Gwen. "You too, Gwen."

She stepped over to me and took my hand, giving it a squeeze. "It's okay, Keira. I'm with you. We know what we saw, right?" Her eyes looked straight into mine and I felt a little better. This was probably the reason Lawrence had asked her to be with me. To stand up to the insanity that was happening right now with my parents.

THIRTY ONE

I walked into the kitchen, as Mom was setting up a fresh pot of coffee. How could she be so....*casual* at a time like this? She'd just laid a bombshell, a crazy one, and now she was just going about putting on fresh coffee? She hadn't even taken her raincoat off.

"So who's this Mr. Thompson? What does he want?"

Her face was impassive when she turned to me. "He's your grandmother's lawyer. She left instructions with him, to be hand delivered."

I looked over to Dad. "What the hell do we need a lawyer for?"

"Because you grandmother left instructions."

I huffed. "Oh. Thanks for clearing that up, Dad." So he knew all about this as well. I wandered over to the kitchen table and had a seat. Gwen was right on my heels, her hand resting on my arm. As odd as it sounds, something about a lawyer showing up added a sense of normalcy to all this.

But the whole visit had been crazy. Only finding out about her, my secret power and then her...I gulped hard. Her death.

Still, I couldn't accept it. "But she was here! So was Lawrence!"

Dad's fingers clasped Mom's arm and he nudged her towards the table. "I'll get the coffee honey. You take a seat."

Mom sat across from Gwen and I. Her eyes were sad when she spoke. "I was with your grandmother when she died. You didn't even know I was gone. Lawrence called me." She sniffed and took a deep breath. "It was a massive heart attack, Keira; we knew her time had come." The tears began to roll down her own cheeks. "She'd told me of her wishes."

"And what were those?"

"To train you, silly. She knew you were at sea—you had no plan for your life. She knew the time was drawing near when you had to learn of your heritage." She gazed around the kitchen, her voice soft. "It's hard to believe but she and Lawrence were able to continue...to materialize long enough for you to learn. She knew you were gifted the first time she held you in the hospital." She covered her face with her hands, and sobbed. "She didn't want to move on until you were ready. And now, my Mama's gone!"

I leaned over the table and my hand covered hers. She may have been trying to be strong earlier, but the grief was like a stone she wore, pulling her down. And as hard as it was for me, it was waaay harder for her. She dropped her hands from her face.

"There was a letter this morning. When I read it, I knew that her time with you was over." Her chin trembled as she looked over to Gwen. "It said Keira would be with her Guardian."

The air drifted from my lungs and I sank lower on the table, my head falling. If only I had known. I would have... A sob rose in my throat and the tears once more flooded my eyes. Nana. It wasn't long enough, the time with you. I never *told* you I loved you.

"But what about Lawrence?" You said he called you to let you know in time for you to see her? What happened to him?" Gwen's voice was soft at my side.

"The night my mother died I got a phone call from the

police. They'd found his body on a park bench near the hospital. There was a note listing me as next of kin. He just gave up living when she died." Mom sniffed. "In many ways he was the father I never knew."

I sat back in my chair like a rag doll, seeing Nana and Lawrence curled up together on her bed the night before. If I'd only known. I would have shook them awake and begged them to stay...if only just a bit longer.

Gwen got up and plucked the box of tissues from the counter. She extended the box to my mother and then to me. As I wiped my tears, she let out a loud honk, blowing her own nose. I smiled over at her, glad that she was there.

I looked across at my mother, who had balled up the tissue in her fist, trying hard to hide the quiver in her chin as she stared out the window. "You knew about all this and still, you sent me here."

She turned to look at me. "It was her last wish, Keira. I didn't know what was going to happen, but I trusted her. I've always known she had a mystical gift. I knew if she wanted you here, there was a good reason. I knew you'd be safe with her."

It was pretty touch and go just yesterday, but I kept that to myself. I rested my chin on my hand. "I'm not the same girl who left New York City last week," I said quietly.

Mom reached out and brushed back my bangs. "No... you're not, are you?"

I nodded. That world was light years away now. "She used to love being in her sun room. She had a pretty good sense of humour. Even when I called her GM, she liked it."

My mother's gaze flashed to me and a smile lit her face. "You called her that? It's a wonder Lawrence didn't throttle you!"

I snorted. "I didn't care for Lawrence at first. That changed when I realized he was the way he was to be protective of her." I looked around the kitchen—his domain. "If you can hear me Lawrence, thank you for everything." I sniffed again. "You old coot."

Dad's gaze rested on Gwen. "And how do you fit into this

crazy scheme? I have a feeling you're into it up to your elbows."

She chuckled. "I liked Keira right off the bat. And the fact that she lived in the old haunted house, just sealed it." She looked over at me. "We're partners in crime now."

"Do you understand what being her Guardian entails?" Mom asked.

"No, not really," she replied. When she saw the look on Mom's face, she added in an even voice, "But I know I can handle it."

The doorbell rang and we all jumped in our chairs.

Mom got to her feet. "That'll be Mr. Thompson."

THIRTY TWO

We left our half empty mugs of coffee on the table, trailing after Mom like ducklings. When she opened the door, a portly man in a suit stared back at her.

"Mr. Thompson, please come in," she said, opening the door wider.

"Mrs. Swanson." He stepped inside. He was carrying a black briefcase the size of a small suitcase.

"I'm so glad you could make it on such short notice."

He glanced around at the rest of us and cleared his throat. "Mrs. York was one of my oldest clients. Of course, I'd reschedule my calendar to make way for this. You have my sincere condolences." His glance took in all of us, once more.

"Will you join us in the dining room? You'll be able to set out your papers there." Mom smiled and extended her hand, signalling the way, before she stepped across the entrance.

I cleared my mind as best I could. I leaned forward to shake his hand. "I'm Mrs. York's granddaughter, Keira." When I took his hand an impression of my grandmother was in his mind. He had genuinely liked Nana. He hoped that I would be as competent as her; but doubted it because I was so young. He was worried I would squander her estate. This was a sharp man who worked eighteen hour days if needed.

"Pleased to meet you, Keira." I followed him and then paused, seeing Gwen hanging back near the door.

"Maybe I'll go now. I mean, this is private...your grandmother's financial affairs and all."

I reached for her hand. "Lawrence wanted you to stay beside me. I want you to stay. If we're going to be in this together, I want to be transparent. There isn't room for secrets, between us. Hell, you shared my last night with my grandmother. Who else would ever believe that?"

She nodded and squeezed my hand.

When we took our place at the table, Mr. Thompson had his large case open and was reaching inside. He brought out two marble urns, one a rose hued one and the other grey, and set them on the sideboard. "Mrs. York's ashes are in the lighter one, while Mr. Brady's are in the grey."

My lips fell apart and an ache so real that it felt like my heart was breaking all over again washed through me. Seeing the evidence was hard. I gazed at my mother and noticed her eyes welling again.

Mr. Thompson reached in his case for a file and took a seat. He opened it and then looked over at my mother and me. "It was your mother and grandmother's wishes that her ashes be spread in the rose garden at the front of the property." He cleared his throat. "The will is very straightforward but I will summarize it before we start. Basically, your trust is to be continued Susan—enough to keep you comfortable for the rest of your life, I'm sure."

I looked over at my parents. So that explained a lot of things. I knew that the diner they ran didn't support them in the lifestyle they led. Nana had been providing for them all these years. The old Keira might have been miffed, considering all the lectures she'd been given about getting a career. But now it made sense. Nana's work had placed her daughter in danger, so of course she'd look out for her financially.

The lawyer's voice captured my attention again. "The rest of Mrs. York's estate is bequeathed to you, Keira. It is yours to do with as you will but Mrs. York's wishes were that you would continue with the financial arrangements she put in place, given that the rate of return has been fortuitous and steady."

I knew about the house but I was curious. "How much is that?"

He took a deep breath and his voice was low. "After taxes, it's eight hundred and forty three million, give or take a few thousand." He tapped the paperwork. "All quite liquid—cash, a blue chip stock portfolio, government bonds, and gold bullion."

Oh my God! I just about fell off my chair and Gwen reached out to steady me. I'd known she was wealthy but this was crazy rich. Wow! That amount was intimidating. I couldn't count that high!

The rest of the will, all legalese went by in an officious drone. My head was still spinning as I signed papers of ownership but under that, my heart was hollow. Sure I was rich, but my grandmother was dead. It had all happened way too fast. There was so much I wanted to know, to learn from her as we lived together. I missed her already.

When my mother and father rose from their chairs, I looked over at the lawyer.

"As I was saying, this next part is for your ears only. Yours and..."His eyes narrowed looking at Gwen. "I'm sorry. You are?"

She froze and gaped at him. "I'm Gwen. Gwen Jones."

He shook his head and his eyebrows arched high. "Mrs. York specified that this next item was to be given only to her granddaughter and 'The Guardian?" He looked over at me.

"That's her. When she'd not delivering mail, that is." I bit my cheeks to keep the chuckle inside. The look on his face was priceless, totally confused. Nana would have loved it!

Mr. Thompson plucked an envelope from the file and handed it to me. "I'm sorry. I am to see that you read it but the contents are for your eyes only."

My parents left the room, closing the door behind them.

I took the envelope and glanced at Gwen as she shifted her chair closer to mine. What the heck was Nana up to now?

THIRTY THREE

Dearest Keira,

Charles Thompson has been a trusted intermediary since I moved to Kingston. The assignments which I have undertaken have come to me from his office. It is one way that I have managed to insulate myself from media and more importantly my adversary. He'll be able to explain to you in greater detail his part in all of this, but please understand he does not know the full details other than I am fascinated with things paranormal.

For this reason, I must stipulate that you continue this arrangement and also that you maintain contact with him, checking in once a week. Often, assignments are related or even occur in the same proximity geographically. It's been an efficient as well as a further control in monitoring my well being.

I would advise that you start out with simple, singular hauntings as opposed to jumping into the fray of multiple entities which are often present in institutional settings such as prisons or hospitals. I have also found that assignments seem to occur in clusters. You may go for weeks or even months with no occurrences and then be bombarded with a few right in a row. Be prepared for these occurrences to happen on, or about the equinox periods. It seems that when the seasons change The Veil becomes diminished. I don't know why.

Remember our lessons in managing fear. Trust in yourself and your Guardian. There are patterns in the Universe that you will become more finely attuned to as you delve deeper into transitioning souls. You already know, there is no such thing as coincidence. It is up to you to discover with your gifts and intuition the why of events.

You are in my thoughts and prayers, always.
With Eternal Love,
Nana

I looked over at Gwen. "What do you think?"

Her head dipped to the side. "I don't know. It's still pretty vague to me. I kind of wish she had spelled out how long these assignments take. I mean, we may be all over the world."

She was worried about her dad. Even though she could ensure his well being with her aunt living with him, she'd still be away for periods of time, when now she spent every day with him. I looked over at Mr. Thompson who was watching us closely. "Do you know, when you gave these...'Assignments' to my grandmother, how long she would be away?"

His eyebrows rose and he sat back. "I take it, we are to continue with the arrangement that your grandmother and I had?"

This was it. I was formally agreeing to take on her role. Now if I could just figure out how it could work out for Gwen. "Yes. But I need more information."

"It varied. She could be gone as little as a few days but at other times, she was gone for a month. She always checked in with me regularly though, whether it was Europe, Asia or

Iceland...anywhere in the world."

Well that was not helpful.

"Do I have to do anything to get her estate transferred to me...bank accounts, her investment portfolio and such?"

He shook his head and smiled. "Most of it was done here today. That's what you pay me for. I will have any final paperwork prepared for your signature in a few days. Until then...well, I'm sure you need some time to adjust to all this." He put the folder back into his case and stood up. When he reached to shake my hand, his eyes were solemn behind the round spectacles. "I'll miss your grandmother. Again, I'm sorry for your loss."

When I went to stand, he shuss'ed me back to my seat. "I can see myself out. I'm sure you and...Gwen, have a lot to talk about."

When the door closed behind him, I turned to Gwen. My heart was in my mouth. If she didn't agree to do this with me, I wasn't sure I'd be able to on my own. "Will you do it? I'll pay you lots of money so you—"

"It's not the money! You know that. It's my dad...and even my *mother* in a weird way. I don't think I can be away from him for long periods. A few days, sure but a month at a time?" Her hand covered mine. "Look I want to but I don't see how it's possible. You know I took this job delivering mail to have more time with him, rather than working long hours in a lab doing research."

"But this is important Gwen. Your dad's important too, don't get me wrong but wouldn't he want you to be happy, doing something like this? Can't you even give it a try before you out and out say no? If my grandmother thought this was a big deal, transitioning in order to protect the order of things, then I don't know how you can turn your back."

"I'm sceptical about all that, Keira."

"What!" Before I could say another word about The Veil, she held up her hand.

"Look, I can accept helping spirits move on, okay? But I really don't want to be responsible for protecting the

Universe." She dropped her hand. "I can't get my head around something like that." She sighed. "Look, I'll think about it, okay? That's as much as I can agree to at this stage."

I sat there dumbfounded. "But... but..."

"That's all I can say, Keira." She sighed. "I'd better get going. You'll be okay with your parents. It'll give you guys a chance to talk."

She got to her feet and I walked with her to the door of the dining room. She turned and gave me a big hug, running her hand softly over my back. "I'm really sorry, Keira, about your grandmother. I wish I could be more definite, but I need time to digest all this. I'm not the type to jump in feet first."

I pulled back and nodded. "Are you going to talk to your dad about all this?" Since it would affect him, he needed to know.

She looked at the ceiling and then shook her head. "There's a good question! I can't tell him everything, now can I? He'd think I lost my mind...having dinner here and the hosts were actually ghosts!" She squeezed my arms. "Sorry, didn't mean to be disrespectful."

The truth was certainly stranger than fiction. It *had* been ever since I'd been summoned to my grandmother's house. "You're right. You'll have to figure something out. Just let me know what you come up with before I see him again."

I opened the door and as we walked to the entry, my parents appeared from the living room.

"You're leaving, Gwen?" My mother walked over and gave Gwen a warm hug. "Thanks for being here for Keira."

Gwen's eyes shot to me and then away quickly. She felt guilty after the conversation we'd just had. "I'm here for her as much as I can be. But I've got to get going to check on my dad."

When the door closed, my father turned to me. "She's a nice girl. I'm glad you had her to turn to today."

"Me too." I just hoped that some kind of miracle would happen that she'd accept the offer I'd made.

"I know you probably don't feel like eating but you should,

Keira. I'll see what's in the freezer and rustle up something for dinner." Mom put her arm over my shoulder and walked me back into the kitchen. She was right about one thing. Even though I hadn't eaten all day, food was the last thing on my mind.

When I took a seat, watching my parents rummaging through the fridge, it hit me. This was a big house and once they left, I'd be pretty lonely. The tears once more welled in my eyes. How could I continue here on my own? The place was too empty without Nana and Lawrence.

I took a deep breath trying to shake off the tears. "How long are you staying?"

THIRTY FOUR

It took two days before we felt up to the task of honouring Nana's last wishes. We took the two urns from the sideboard and went out to the front yard, to the rose that always bloomed. Gwen had taken a sick day to be with us. It was the first that I'd seen her since we'd learned the news about Nana and Lawrence.

Now here we were on a brilliant summer day, the four of us standing in a circle around the flower bed. That red rose bush was covered with flowers in various stages, from buds to spent blooms that drifted down to the dark earth.

Mom stepped close to the brick wall and lifted the top from Lawrence's gray urn. As she poured his ashes to the base of the plant, a tear rolled down her cheek. "Goodbye Lawrence, old friend. I know you're with Pamela, your one true love." She sobbed and added, "My mother. May you find peace and happiness for all time."

She turned to me. I held my grandmother's urn close to my chest. Even though it was her wish to join with the rose, I clung to her essence. A monarch butterfly landed on the wall, its orange wings completely still. The last time I'd noticed a butterfly was the day I was expelled from the acting school. I'd taken it as a harbinger of good will at that time. Was it a sign from Nana, now?

I stepped forward and my vision was blurry as I removed the top of the urn and set it on the wall. "Goodbye Nana. I'm glad I spent the time with you. I love you." My shoulders wracked as I tipped the urn.

My father stepped over between my mother and I and his arms went over our shoulders.

"Goodbye Pamela and Lawrence," he said.

"Farewell, Mrs. York, Lawrence," said Gwen.

I sniffed and then we dispersed, turning to go back into the house. Mom and Dad went into the kitchen while I led Gwen to the sun room. It seemed a fitting place to talk about serious matters.

She wandered around the room, touching and sniffing the plants that lined the shelves. "This really is a beautiful spot."

"Yeah. It was her favourite place, that's for sure." I could almost see her sitting in the wicker chair across the table when I took my usual spot. I took a deep breath. "So, have you come to any decision?" I realized how cold that was and quickly added. "I'm sorry; how is your dad?"

"He's great." She took a seat next to me, leaning close. "I told him that your grandmother and Lawrence died. He knows there was a private ceremony today and sends his condolences. He just doesn't know it was weeks ago."

It was hard to sit so patiently when my future was so dependent on what she would say next.

"I told him that your grandmother was really rich. That she has business interests all over the world and that she often travelled to them." She smiled and rolled her eyes. "I hate lying. I don't think I'm all that good at it. I also told him that you are going to continue doing that...checking up on your grandmother's businesses."

"Do you think he bought it?"

"I'm not sure but he didn't ask too many questions. It was

only when I told him that you wanted me to go with you that he surprised me. He insisted that I take you up on it. He's always wanted to travel and he told me I was a fool to walk away from it. He even came up with the same idea that I had—for Aunt Elizabeth to retire in Kingston and live with him."

As she spoke, I stopped breathing in case I'd jinx this. Devon was totally on side with this! This was going to work!

She saw the excitement on my face and her smile dropped. "I arranged for a six month leave of absence from work. I'll try this but I need to know if it's too hard on me not seeing Dad as much, that I've got a job to go back to."

I grasped her arm barely able to keep from popping out of my chair. "It'll work! I just know it. But I respect that it's on a trial basis. You know, if your Aunt comes to live with your dad and you don't get along with her, there's plenty of room in this house for you!" The house was way too big even for two people.

Her hand rose. "Hold on! One step at a time. I'll call Aunt Elizabeth tonight. I'm not even sure she'll do it!"

"Does she know about the household allowance? That will tempt her." My mind was working overtime.

"What allowance? There's Dad's disability and my earnings, that's about all."

"Wanna bet?" I waggled my eyebrows. "The allowance that is going to make its way to your father's bank account. Ten thousand a month should let them live comfortably don't you think?"

"Keira! He'd never accept that!"

"Say you won it in the lottery then! You'll think of something. And as for you, will a cool mill a year be enough to get by on?"

Her mouth fell open and she blinked. "That's too much." She grinned. "But…on the other hand, I'll just suck it up and deal with it." She put the back of her hand to her forehead. "Now I'm going to be really bitching about paying taxes!"

We both had a laugh and I sat back and looked around the room. Everything was falling into place. There was just one other thing....

"You know, I haven't been out of this house except to see you, since I've been here. I spent a week with my dead grandmother and her dead companion and before that I was kicked out of school and then banished by my parents! I need a vacation!"

Gwen's face lit up and she laughed. "Oh yeah? Where are you going to go?"

"Unh unh. Where are WE going to go? It's no fun going alone." The more I thought of it, the more I could sense that Nana would approve. It was time to join the living before we took on the job of the dead.

My mother and father strolled into the room and seeing the looks on our faces, they smiled.

"What's going on? You two are up to something." My dad held out my Nana's chair for my mother to take a seat.

"Gwen and I are taking a vacation."

"Hold on! I never agreed. I'd have to call my brother and get him to come down from Toronto. And then—"

"I'm seeing me on a beach drinking Mai Tai's, the liquor cool and the guys hot."

My mother's face flushed pink. "Ewwww! Parents here!"

Gwen shook her head. "Not a fan of the beach. After the first day that would be boring. I like to get around and see historical things. That's my idea of fun."

I swatted her arm playfully. She was considering this! "The beach, baby!"

Dad leaned over the table and grinned. "Why not do both? The Mayan Riviera has awesome beaches and is packed with history. You should go!"

"They have pyramids there, you know," Gwen said.

"The Mayan Riviera's in Egypt?" I asked. The rest of them burst out laughing. "What? What's so funny?"

Mom made a small wave with her hand. "Nothing, dear; sometimes you're silly, that's all." Mom reached into the pocket of her blouse and placed a small white box on the table. "I had this made for you Keira. Actually I had one made for myself as well." She pushed the box towards me.

I opened it and lifted a gold tear-shaped pendant with a loop of gold chain. I lifted it out and looked at it closely.

"Some of your grandmother's ashes are embedded in it. She'll always be with you." Mom reached over and her hand covered mine. Grinning, she arched an eyebrow. "She'd always liked the Mayan Riviera."

My fingers closed around the small tear drop. Nana would always be with me.

The End

AUTHOR'S NOTE

Yes, there are more adventures in store for Keira and Gwen, don't worry! I'm currently finishing up the second book in this series. These characters have grown on me, and writing the farewell note from GM was a deeply moving experience. Thank you for reading this book, I truly hope you enjoyed it. Many, many hours went into its creation. Not only by myself, but also on the part of those near and dear to me. If you enjoyed it, please leave a review for it on Amazon. Honest reviews from readers such as yourself help authors, yes; but more importantly, your voice helps other readers a great deal in making their decisions.

ABOUT THE AUTHOR

A lifelong resident of Kingston, Ontario, Michelle has experienced firsthand, eerie events. She's witnessed episodes where the veil between our world and the next has shimmered gossamer thin. These encounters fascinate rather than frighten her. On the other hand, her two pugs Ruby and Sookie freak out enough for the three of them. The Irish part of her heritage, stories of banshees, druids and, yes, leprechauns are what started her down the road of writing about the paranormal.

In the summer she dreams about skiing, and in the winter wishes she lived in Cuba. Yes, she's contrary as hell, but never boring. She hopes you enjoy reading her work as much as she enjoys writing it. She is currently practicing her acceptance speech for the Nobel Prize in Literature just in case.

OTHER WORKS BY THE AUTHOR

THE HAUNTINGS OF KINGSTON

Crawley House
The Haunted Inn
The Ghosts of Centre Street
The Haunting Of Larkspur Farm
The Ghosts of Hanson House

THE MYSTICAL VEIL

Legacy
Heritage

Made in the USA
Monee, IL
10 May 2020

30189669R00128